FAITH FULL

By VINCE AIELLO

Published by SarEth Publishing House
SarEth Publishing House
Carlsbad, California

This novel is a work of fiction. All names, characters, places, and incidents are fictitious and purely the work of the author's imagination. Any similarities to any actual person, living or dead, places, or events are purely coincidental.

Cover Photography & Photo Editing © 2015 Sarah Rose Aiello
Armorer Advisor: Ethan P. Aiello

Bible excerpts within this novel are taken from the New American Bible (Revised Edition) (2010) and the King James Version (1987).

First Edition: April 2015

Printed in the United States of America

ISBN 978-0-9883413-6-4

SPHN 15-1115200806

SarEth Publishing House

Also by Vince Aiello

LEGAL DETRIMENT

THE LITIGATION GUY

LEGION'S LAWYERS

*For **Fr. Don Coleman** & **Fr. Bill Marquis** –Priests that make you think. Great teachers and great preachers.*

What I am doing, you do not understand now,
but you will understand later.

-John 13:7

PROLOGUE

SEMANY WHOLESALE FLOWERS WAREHOUSE
CARLSBAD, CALIFORNIA

Carlsbad, California is an affluent, seaside resort city located on a seven mile stretch of the coastline of the Pacific Ocean in Northern San Diego County. It is approximately ninety miles south of Los Angeles and thirty-five miles north of downtown San Diego. It is the home of LEGOLAND in the United States and considered a premier tourist destination.

As night blanketed the city, the only source of natural illumination came from a full moon. There were no stars in the sky and its stillness gave off an innate sense of faux beauty. The street was dotted with a spattering of street lights and the traffic light at the intersection of Faraday Avenue and Van Allen Way stood like a lonely sentinel awaiting vehicles to control. The temperature was 62 degrees Fahrenheit and a cool breeze wafted up Faraday Avenue from the Pacific Ocean, more than a mile away.

The Semany Wholesale Flowers warehouse sat on an eight acre lot on the southwest corner of Faraday Avenue and Van Allen Way. The building was a two-story wood and metal structure with an age of more than thirty years. For most of that time, it was one of the few buildings in this area. The company that ran the business closed their doors five years earlier. The property was for sale and the building was occasionally rented out on a part-time basis.

Since the late 1990s, this part of Carlsbad had blossomed into a technology center and nearly every parcel of land had been christened with an office building.

The bland, canary yellow warehouse had 100,000 square feet of space. The south side of the building opposite Faraday Avenue was lined with overhead doors to allow tractor-trailers to enter.

On each side of the building was a parking lot with enough room to allow a tractor-trailer to maneuver. There was a public entrance on the north side of the building and two metal doors on the western side of the structure. These doors were only accessible to those exiting the building. They each had a door lock, but no door handle and the hinges were recessed into the doorframe. There was also a door adjacent to the line of overhead doors, which had an intercom system to allow visitors ingress into the building.

At this time of night, there were at least ten police cars from the Carlsbad Police Department and the San Diego County Sheriff's Department investigating a crime scene.

Earlier that day, during the noon hour, the building had been visited by police officers.

Detectives Wayne Patterson and Andy Sandoval of the Carlsbad Police Department were waiting for a signature on a search warrant while discussing strategy to enter the building with Captain Ross Hardiman of the SWAT unit. Wayne was 55 years old, 5 feet 9 inches tall, with a slender, but sturdy build. His hair was thick and gray; combed back with just a tinge of black. He wore black Haggar slacks, a white shirt, and a black and blue striped tie. His attire was complimented with a gray herringbone sport coat that was two sizes larger than the actual size, to assist in concealing his Smith and Wesson M & P 40 caliber semi-automatic handgun.

Andy Sandoval was 36 years old, 5 feet 10 inches tall, with a husky build and obvious upper body strength. He had black hair, bald on top and wore glasses with tortoise shell frames, giving him an intellectual appearance. He wore a navy blazer, gray slacks with a gray and blue windowpane shirt and a loose fitting solid, blue tie.

The plan was for three teams of SWAT officers – X-ray, Yankee, and Zulu – to watch the front entrance door and the two doors on the western side of the building. Detectives Patterson and Sandoval would enter through the door adjacent to the overhead doors backed up by two uniformed officers.

Down the street on Van Allen Way, the SWAT team's Lenco Bearcat armored transport vehicle, complete with a mechanical rotating turret, stood ready to enter the fray at a moment's notice.

"What do you think is in there, Wayne?" SWAT Captain Hardiman inquired of Detective Patterson.

"I don't know, but I've got a bad feeling about it," Wayne responded as he gazed upon the building.

Wayne had been a Carlsbad police officer for the past thirty-two years. He was the longest tenured member of the department. He was also a former SWAT team leader and all the members of the SWAT team respected him as an authority figure.

Wayne suddenly turned his gaze to his partner, Detective Sandoval.

"Andy, call and find out where that warrant. . ."

Before Wayne finished his sentence, one of the metal doors, located twenty feet from where they were standing suddenly burst open with a young girl screaming in terror and exigent to exit the building. She looked like she may have been fifteen years old, but she was actually twenty-two years old, 4 feet 10 inches tall, and 91 pounds. She had shoulder-length, blonde hair, a blue and white flannel shirt, denim skirt, and a t-shirt that simply said, in cursive writing, 'THAT'S HOW I ROLL!'

She hit the door so hard to escape that she was slightly discombobulated by her impact with it. The door immediately slammed shut behind her. A look of realization came over Wayne's face as he recognized her.

"Chelbi," Wayne called out and she promptly focused on his voice. She was Chelbi Gorringe, the granddaughter of one of Wayne's closest friends.

She ran to him hysterical, crying, and wanting to be hugged for a split second. She took a step back to look at him through her tears.

"Oh, my God, you've got to help him! They're gonna kill him!" Her message was urgent as she spoke with a cracking voice.

"Who?" Wayne responded with matched urgency.

"Nice," she responded, trying to hold back uncontrollable crying.

"Nicean?" Wayne asked, knowing that she was referring to a young man named Nicean 'Nice' Bevilacqua.

"We were trying to help these girls in there."

As Chelbi completed her sentence, the unmistakable sound of a shotgun blast was heard from inside the building. Its resonance left a deadly pall over the landscape.

"Oh, God, they killed him!" she uttered with frenzied convulsion and a tempest of tears.

Like a quick cut in a movie, Wayne looked to the building and then back to SWAT Captain Hardiman.

"Give me your shotgun." It was not a request, it was a command.

Captain Hardiman was hesitant, but handed him the weapon. It was loaded with Disintegrator breaching rounds capable of destroying deadbolts, locks, and hinges.

"Wayne, wait!" Hardiman cautioned as Wayne walked to the door that Chelbi exited.

"Chelbi," Wayne told her as he stopped for a moment. "Stay with this detective," he said pointing to his partner, Andy Sandoval.

Wayne took the shotgun and moved briskly toward the building. As he approached it, he racked the shotgun by pumping it once. When he was within three feet of the door, he fired three shots at the door in quick succession, pumping it each time and turning his head away with each blast. The first blast was aimed at the locking mechanism of the door and the next two shots were aimed at the hinges of the door. Each shot blew apart its intended target. Wayne took one final shot at the center of the door, which blew the door and the doorframe into the building.

As Wayne rushed into the building, Captain Hardiman ordered the three SWAT teams to make entry.

Wayne entered a darkened loading area where tractor-trailers would normally be parked. The smell of fresh cut flowers, in particular, lilies-of-the-valley permeated the air. There were several parked vehicles at the far end of the building, including a brown, Oldsmobile Toronado. Wayne could hear the other SWAT teams make entry and begin the process of clearing the building for any unfriendly combatants.

Darkness enveloped the room. In the center of the loading area, approximately fifty feet from the door where Wayne entered stood Nice Bevilacqua. The sunlight shined down on Nice's 6 foot 3 inch solid frame and blond hair like a spotlight through the only skylight in the ceiling. He looked confused and dirty, with a line of dried blood on his left cheek.

Wayne's voice refocused him.

"Nicean," Wayne called out. As he did, the other SWAT team members took aim at Nice and six red, laser dots filled his chest.

"Hold your fire!" Wayne yelled. "Get the lights!"

Wayne could see that Nice was holding something in his hand.

"Nice. What's in your hand?"

"My roadmap," he timidly responded.

"Drop it!" Wayne ordered.

Nice let go of the book in his hand and his Bible fell to the ground. As it fell, the lights came on, flooding the room with bright, clear illumination.

Less than ten feet from where Nice stood, lay the bodies of seven men holding various handguns and one man holding a shotgun. Their condition was unknown, but they were not moving. Wayne could see that Nice wore a blue t-shirt that had a hole in the center of the chest in the front and back of it. The back of the shirt appeared to be blood-soaked.

"Are you all right?" Wayne inquired with a concerned, elevated voice as he lowered his shotgun and began a slow creep toward Nice.

"Yeah," Nice answered.

"What happened here?"

Nice slowly perused the bodies and surveyed the carnage. He then turned to Wayne.

"A miracle."

Part 1

CHAPTER 1

7 DAYS EARLIER

On this Good Friday, two days before Easter, an overflow crowd of more than five hundred visitors filled the pews of Saint Elizabeth Seton Catholic Church in Carlsbad, California to standing room only. The church, built in 1995, stood as a monument to architectural awe and reverential beauty. It was adorned with slate, cherry wood, and magnificent detailed icons of two thousand years of faith.

Nicean Bevilacqua and his mother, Sally, sat in the third row from the back of the church. They arrived more than an hour before the service began to make sure they would get a good parking space and a good seat.

On Sally's arm sat her seven pound, black and gray, toy schnauzer terrier named Yappy. Yappy was never left alone and he accompanied Sally to church every day. The dog never uttered a sound in church and remained quiet unless a stranger came within three feet of Sally. When this occurred, Yappy turned into the werewolf of Carlsbad.

Sally was 57 years old, 5 feet 1 inch tall and weighed 120 pounds. Her hair was colored black with a pixie cut and she wore a gray, piped sheath dress with a black sweater and glasses with an aqua blue frame.

Nice wore a blue suit on his 6 foot 3 inch frame, with a white shirt and red and blue striped tie. Nice weighed 195 pounds with close-cropped, blond hair combed to the side and was clean-shaven.

Next to Nice was his employer, Ben Krische, and his wife, Theresa. Ben was 68 years old, 5 feet 11 inches tall, and 260 pounds. He moved slowly, due to crippling arthritis, and a simple sense of being wobbly on his feet. When he stood, he was noticed for his imposing frame. But he was always in a good mood and genuinely happy to see everyone. In college, Ben was a defensive end at the University of Kansas at Topeka. He wore a black suit that was slightly snug on him, with a white shirt and a loose fitting yellow tie. He wore reading glasses, but still needed to squint to see various prayers.

Ben was the proprietor of Ben's Glassworks, a Carlsbad institution for more than forty years. He was always in the mood for a dish of ice cream or a piece of cake. His daily insulin injections served as a testament to his love for all foods that were enhanced by sugar.

Ben's wife, Theresa or Terry, was 68 years old, 110 pounds and always smiling. She wore navy slacks with a dark, silk popover blouse and a blue sweater.

The pastor of Saint Elizabeth Seton Church was Father Thomas Hayes. He was 65 years old, 6 feet tall, 200 pounds, with thick, white hair, glasses, and a craggy face. His red vestments served as a reminder of the solemnity of the occasion and the commemoration of the brutal beating and death suffered by Jesus Christ.

One of the main readings of every Catholic mass is referred to as the Gospel. These are readings authored by the Evangelists:

Matthew, Mark, Luke, and John and tell the story of Jesus Christ's time on earth. This day's Gospel would be a dramatic reading dealing with the crucifixion and death of Jesus Christ as relayed by John. This particular reading, often referred to as the Passion in Christianity, was unique in that it involved role-playing on the part of the congregants. Father Hayes would respond as Jesus, there would be a narrator, and all of the church members would respond as the crowd.

Nice had always been disturbed by this reading for as long as he could remember. He was homeschooled by his mother and every day she included a Bible reading that would be discussed and analyzed. If Sally was unable to explain any passage sufficiently, she would seek guidance from either a Bible study teacher at church or from Father Hayes.

The same Gospel reading had been done the Sunday before, Palm Sunday, but that passage was authored by the Evangelist Matthew.

What troubled Nice was the portion of the passage where the Roman governor, Pontius Pilate, asked the crowd who he should release – Jesus or Barabbas, a notorious criminal.

The crowd, in this case, the church attendees, are to say in unison that they want Barabbas released and they want Jesus crucified.

Nice knew that he would never respond this way under any circumstance. In the past, he would simply refuse to answer when the crowd spoke. But today, he was moved to action.

"Which of the two do you want me to release to you?" queried Detective Wayne Patterson as he read the part of Pilate.

As the crowd responded, "Barabbas!" Nice simultaneously bellowed at the top of his lungs.

"JESUS! RELEASE JESUS!"

Sally grabbed his sleeve to pull him down, but he would not move. Ben, Theresa, and even Yappy looked at him in amazement. Sally's face turned from astonished to percolated anger.

Wayne did not wish to bring additional attention to Nice's outburst. He continued with the reading unfazed.

"Then what should I do with Jesus called Christ?" Wayne asked.

"Let him be crucified!" was the crowd's response.

"NO!" Nice responded with petulant ire. "He did nothing to deserve to be crucified! We can't condone evil!"

Everyone in the church was now staring at Nice. Nice stared back at them wondering what they could not understand. A shroud of silence engulfed the church. Ben reached over and tugged on Nice's coat sleeve. Nice looked down at Ben, who shook his head slightly in a negative fashion.

"I'm sorry." Nice conveyed his mea culpa to the silent crowd. "Please forgive me."

Nice sat down and glanced at his mother. He knew from the look on her face that she was going to be talking about this moment for the next several hours, if not the next several days.

The service concluded and Sally wanted to be one of the last people out of the church. Ben and Theresa also liked to wait for most of the crowd to leave because Ben moved slowly and did not want to obstruct others from leaving church. As Sally rose to leave, she saw Wayne walking toward the narthex of the church.

"Wayne," Sally called out. "Would you come here, please? Nice has something he wants to say to you."

Wayne greeted Nice with a firm handshake.

"Peace be with you," Nice began with his standard greeting. "I wanted to apologize for disrupting your reading. I'm sorry."

"No problem," Wayne smiled. "At least you were listening."

Wayne then shared a handshake with Ben.

"You're coming over Sunday, right?' Ben asked with elation in his voice. "At least for coffee and cake?"

"Marion and I will be there," Wayne answered referring to his wife. "What's the chef-girl-ar-dee making?"

"Pumpkin cheesecake," Theresa replied.

"What's everybody else gonna have?" Ben gleefully replied as if he was laying claim to the entire cheesecake. His comment brought a smile to everyone.

"Come on," Sally told Nice. "There's one other person you have to talk to."

When Sally was assertive with Nice, the image was almost comical. He was more than a foot taller than she was, but when she spoke with a stern voice, he was as attentive as a private to a drill sergeant.

"Please, ma," Nice begged, knowing that it would be useless.

Sally stopped and yanked on Nice's arm to force him to look at her.

"What is the first commandment with a promise in it?" she asked through grinding teeth.

"Honor thy father and mother," Nice responded without expression in a tone of surrender.

"What does Colossians three, twenty say?" she asked with an angered voice.

"Children, obey your parents in all things: for this is well pleasing unto the Lord," Nice responded, not looking her in the eye.

"Okay, so think about it next time you want to go off on a Tarzan rant in front of the whole church. You know how upset your sister gets when anybody raises their voice. And I don't want Yappy upset."

Sally referred to her dog, Yappy, as Nice's sister and Nice was considered Yappy's brother. In their home, they did not consider Yappy to be an animal, but rather a member of their family.

As they headed to the church exit, Father Hayes was greeting the congregants and wishing them a happy Easter. Ben and his wife, along with Nice and his mother, waited in line for their opportunity to speak with the priest. While waiting, Nice and Ben chatted for a moment.

"I'm sorry, Ben," Nice conveyed apologetically.

"No need," Ben retorted. "You spoke your mind. That's what a man does. I'm proud of you."

That interaction exemplified the nature of Ben and Nice's relationship. Nice's father died before he was one year old and Ben had stepped into the role of a surrogate father to him. He taught Nice a skill, taught him how to drive, gave him a company truck to take home at night and a company credit card. No matter what adversity ever came Nice's way, Ben always made it disappear with his wisdom and positive attitude.

"Hey," Ben added, "my granddaughter is coming into town tomorrow. Can you give me a ride down to the airport?"

"Sure. What time?"

"Her plane gets here at 2:45," Theresa chimed in.

"Okay. I'll pick you up about an hour before," Nice told him.

As Nice finished his sentence, it was now his turn to speak with Father Hayes. They met with a strong handshake.

"Peace be with you, Father. I'm sorry about my outburst. I got caught up in the moment."

"I know your concerns are heartfelt and truly appreciated," Father Hayes told him. "But you've got to remember, there can be no joy of Easter Sunday without the thorns of Good Friday. It's unfortunate, but it had to happen."

In his mind, Nice was unable to accept that statement. He also knew that this was not the time to debate a priest on this topic. Nice believed that there was something he could do about it. He wasn't sure what it was, but he was going to find out.

CHAPTER 2

The Palomar Medical Center located on Citracado Parkway in Escondido, California in the northwest corner of San Diego County was considered one of the most technologically advanced hospitals in the United States when it opened in August of 2012.

The hospital was eleven stories high, contained 288 private, single-patient rooms, 44 emergency and trauma rooms, and 11 operating rooms, all on a 56 acre campus.

In room 601, at 6:30 pm, Marion Patterson sat quietly as she held the hand of her daughter, Joy, who lay motionless in a hospital bed. Joy was 24 years old, slender, frail, and without hair or eyebrows from chemotherapy treatments. Her facial expression was neither happy nor sad. It was merely one of existence.

The sounds that filled the antiseptic clean room were the machines that monitored her vital signs, particularly for blood pressure and pulse. In her arm was a catheter connected to an intra-venous saline solution to keep her hydrated. On the right side of her chest, above her breast, was another catheter, referred to as a 'PICC line,' which allowed chemotherapy drugs into her system during treatment.

Marion was 54 years old, 5 feet 4 inches tall, and weighed 150 pounds. She wore a baroque, floral scrolled band-collar blouse, black Italian flannel tailored ankle pants, a white, button sweater, and black, ballet flat shoes. Her smile was a beacon of kindness and compassion. She always found the glass half full and always anticipated the best in human nature from everyone.

Marion had married her husband, Detective Wayne Patterson, thirty-four years earlier, after they met during a college social event in Dubuque, Iowa. Wayne would always tell her that he knew he was going to marry her within ten seconds after he first laid eyes upon her. For every moment thereafter, he knew that he made the right decision.

Marion stood next to the bed and looked down at her only child.

"Do you want anything, honey?" Marion asked with a kind, reassuring voice.

"Where's daddy?" she answered, in a weakened state, struggling with each word.

"He's on his way."

Marion held her hand and gently rubbed the back of it. Joy's expression did not change. Then, Wayne appeared in the doorway.

"Hi, girls," Wayne exclaimed, trying to bring some cheer to the room. He walked over to the opposite side of the bed from Marion.

"How is she?" he asked.

"The same," Marion replied, trying to remain as positive as possible.

"Daddy," Joy's frail voice uttered.

"Yeah, baby, I'm right here."

"Do you remember when we went to the opening day at LEGOLAND?"

"I do. It was in 1999."

"March 20, 1999."

"I remember there were a lot of people," Wayne asserted matter-of-factly.

"But we went back every year until I went to college." As Joy finished her sentence, she started to cough almost uncontrollably. Marion raced to grab a glass of water and Wayne held up her head as she took a sip.

"Listen, pretty princess," Wayne declared, "we're gonna go again."

"I don't think I can see," she conveyed with sadness.

"Don't worry about it, babe. Every time your mother went on the rides, she always closed her eyes. At least you can remember what they look like," Wayne continued his effort to put forth a positive front.

"They're just as scary with your eyes closed," Marion added.

"Read me a verse, daddy," Joy requested. Ever since she was a little girl, she would turn the pages on their Bible to a random section for her father to read aloud and discuss.

Marion retrieved her Bible, opened it and placed it on the bed, then placed Joy's hand upon it. Joy moved the pages with her fingers until she stopped and pointed down on the page. Wayne then lifted the book, making sure that he did not lose the location she selected.

"All right," he said adjusting his eyeglasses. "This is Mark, chapter 5, verse 23," he advised as he realigned his eyes. "*And besought him greatly, saying, my little daughter lieth at the point of death.*" Wayne looked up dumbfounded and disconcerted by his daughter's selection. He looked down and continued, "*I pray thee, come and lay thy hands on her, that she may be healed; and she shall live.*"

Wayne and Marion looked at each other in a nonplussed manner and both knew exactly what the other was thinking. Was Joy's selection an act of serendipity or was it something else?

CHAPTER 3

In a murky studio apartment, located over an aged garage situated just off Laguna Drive in downtown Carlsbad, its lone occupant sat in the darkness awaiting a phone call. The windows were covered with blankets and only thin, slivers of light were able to pierce through around the edges where the blankets failed to completely cover the windows.

The room smelled dusty and the furniture consisted of a broken down couch, which also served as a bed, one kitchen chair, a rusty card table, and a rocking chair with a cracked seat.

The man sat still on the couch wearing blue jeans and no shirt, just looking forward. His torso and arms were completely filled with tattoos. The tattoos rose up to cover a portion of his neck and his bald head. A flip phone sat on the couch cushion next to him. When it began to ring, he calmly picked it up and looked at the Caller ID. He opened the phone and brought it up to the side of his head.

"Hello," the resident answered with a raspy voice.

"Mr. Molech?" came a voice through the phone.

"Yes," was his reply.

"This is Mr. Feardesin. Have the targets been identified?"

"Yes."

"Will the targets be obtained pursuant to the timeline we discussed?"

"Yes."

"The transport vehicle will be there on Friday," the voice advised devoid of emotion.

"Very good."

"I wish to remind you that I have no interest in purchasing damaged goods."

"They won't be damaged," Molech assured him with eerie gruffness.

"Good," answered the voice. "Don't disappoint me. You know what I am capable of."

With that, the caller ended the conversation. Mr. Molech closed the phone and returned it to the couch cushion. He rose from the couch and maneuvered his 6 foot 4 inch, 230 pound frame quickly through the darkened room. From the card table, he retrieved a wig of curly, black hair. A portion of his skull appeared to be concave and the wig covered the area nicely. He then picked up an eye patch and placed it over his left eye. The cornea of his left eye was clouded and milky. A scar ran down his forehead through the center of his left eye and down his left cheek.

It was time to assemble his team and hunt for prey.

CHAPTER 4

The late model, Ford F-150, white pickup truck, complete with the Ben's Glassworks logo on each door, drove through the arrival lanes of Terminal 2 of the San Diego Airport. Nice and Ben were there to pick up Ben's granddaughter, Chelbi, who was arriving from Topeka, Kansas. They were searching for the American Airlines doors and when Nice spotted them, he parked the truck along the curb in front of them.

"Do you think we can stop here?" Nice wondered.

"Sure," Ben was quick to reply. "I brought my handicap placard. You go inside and get her. She should be at the luggage carousel. I'll wait with the truck."

"Here's the keys," Nice announced as he removed them to hand to Ben.

"Leave'em in the ignition. You know what she looks like, right?"

"Yeah. Theresa showed me a picture."

"All right. I'll move the truck if I have to," Ben assured him.

"If there's a problem, call me," Nice's request evidenced his genuine concern.

"Don't worry. Now go."

Nice stepped out of the truck and moved briskly to a series of luggage carousels inside the terminal. He found the carousel that contained the luggage from Chelbi's flight and saw people retrieving their bags.

He spotted a little girl, 4 feet 10 inches tall, 91 pounds, with blonde, shoulder-length hair, parted in the middle, wearing blue jeans, sneakers, and a fluorescent green windbreaker that was zipped up to her neck. Even though she appeared to be the size of a young teenager, she was 22 years old. She was having difficulty lifting her large bag off the carousel and kept dragging it against the other bags.

Nice walked right up to the carousel, where Chelbi was leaning over, and lifted the bag, taking it from Chelbi's hand.

"Thank you," she said, looking up at his considerable stature and waiting for him to either put the bag down or give it to her.

"You're welcome. Peace be with you," Nice told her, which was his standard response when he met anyone.

Chelbi was slightly put off by his response and hoped that he was not going to ask her for money. It was followed by a moment of awkward silence. She went to reach for the bag and Nice pulled it back.

"I'll carry it," he told her.

"I don't need any help."

"I'm a friend of your grandfather. I'm here to pick you up."

"Okay," she said surveying him. "But I can handle my own bag. What's your name?"

"I'm Nice."

"Huh," she laughed slightly. "Well, so am I, but what's your name?"

"My name is Nicean, but I go by Nice."

"Well that's different," she stated matter-of-factly. "I'm Chelbi."

"It's a pleasure to meet you, Chelbi. Your grandfather is waiting for us out at the curb," Nice told her and they walked to the exit doors with Nice carrying her large, oversized suitcase.

Chelbi did not know if Nice was a good guy, a prince, or a weirdo. She needed more time to evaluate him. She got the vibe that he wasn't a partier and that could be a problem.

CHAPTER 5

As the sun was setting on this Saturday night Easter Eve, Nice took the opportunity to take a seat on his patio deck and appreciate the sunset. The Pacific Ocean was less than a mile from the duplex he shared with his mother and he observed the sun setting into it with a panoply of different colored hues that created a magnificent display. The temperature was 68 degrees Fahrenheit and a light zephyr blew in from the ocean.

Nice was always in awe of the majestic beauty of nature and he would often ponder what it must have taken to create it.

Nice's condominium did not have its own backyard, but rather a shared common area. His patio deck was ten feet by ten feet, with two chairs, a large umbrella for shade, and a propane barbeque.

Nice heard the sounds of scratching on the screen door of the sliding glass door that allowed entrance to the house. He turned and saw Yappy scratching for attention and an exit.

"Nice, your sister wants to talk to you," Sally's voice suddenly filled the doorway and she slid the screen door to allow Yappy onto the patio. "I need bread for your lunch on Monday.

You want to go down to Ralphs?" she inquired referring to the closest grocery store.

"Ma," Nice answered in frustration and stood to speak with her. "I told you that I don't want you to make my lunch. I want to have lunch with the guys at work."

"You know how expensive that is?" Sally's retort was quick. "And all they eat is fast food, right?"

"So, what? I'm getting paid and most of the time Ben treats everybody."

"Even at a fast food place, it's probably seven or eight dollars. We need every dollar to make our bills around here. And why should Ben have to pay?"

"He offers." Nice was flummoxed by her stubbornness.

"Nicean, I will be making your lunch for Monday," Sally announced definitively. "Please go get me a loaf of bread."

"All right," Nicean capitulated as he surrendered to her. "I'll go in a few minutes."

Nice returned to his chair and Yappy stood on her back legs, doing a slight dance, indicating that she wanted to be picked up.

"What are you doing, little girl?" he asked Yappy as he lifted her and placed her in his lap. Yappy then stood in his lap and he held her with Yappy's butt in the crook of his arm and he rubbed her back with his other hand. Yappy took the opportunity to lick him excessively on the cheek.

Nice continued to be plagued by his outburst in church and how easily the church members would respond that they wanted Christ crucified. It was at that moment, with Yappy in his arms and mesmerized by the sunset on the Pacific Ocean, that Nice had an epiphany.

He realized that if he could go back in time and literally put the 'fear of God' in those people who wanted to crucify Christ, he could change the outcome. To do this, all Nice would need is a time machine and a weapon that he would not use to kill, but only to intimidate.

Then it came to him: To help Jesus on that day, he would need to find a time machine and a machine gun.

"Yappy, I know what I have to do."

At sun up, his mission would begin.

CHAPTER 6

Ben lived in an affluent area of Carlsbad, referred to as Aviara. The homes were newer with well-manicured lawns and surrounded by lush foliage.

Ben and Theresa's home was a single story, three thousand square foot, Spanish-style home, approximately 12 years old. They had moved to this location from a larger home as Ben was realizing at the time that he wanted to downsize and he did not want to go up and down stairs any longer.

On this Easter day, Sally, Nice and Yappy arrived at Ben's home at approximately 1:00 pm after attending morning mass and having an opportunity to change into casual clothes. Yappy really enjoyed Ben's house because it was an opportunity to go on searching adventures and Ben had a bed, food dish, water dish, and assorted dog toys available for her. He also knew the kind of dog treats she enjoyed and made sure they were always available.

While Sally assisted Theresa with the preparation of the meal, Nice went into research mode. He really did not know where to begin. On a bottom shelf of a bookcase was a set of World Book Encyclopedias. There was a chair situated next to the bookcase and this was where Nice took up residence. The problem was that this set of encyclopedias had a copyright date of 1962. They were able to detail information about the then, current president, John F. Kennedy.

After two hours, Nice was frustrated with his lack of success. All he could find regarding a time machine or time travel was a reference to the H.G. Wells novel, *The Time Machine*, published in 1898. Yappy poked his leg several times for attention and Nice picked her up and set her on his lap.

"Nice, where's your sister?" Sally's raised voice inquired from the kitchen.

"She's in my lap," he responded, not giving it much thought and continuing to peruse the pages.

"Take her outside," Sally requested. "She probably has to go potty. Then it's time to eat."

Nice returned the encyclopedia that he was reading to its place on the shelf, then he and Yappy exited to Ben's backyard through the sliding glass door. There was a large patio with a table, four chairs surrounding it, and a large umbrella to cast shade.

Nice set Yappy down and did not notice Chelbi at first, sitting at the table facing the backyard.

"Hi," Nice told her. "Peace be with you."

"You told me that yesterday," Chelbi answered not breaking her gaze at the manicured landscape.

"It probably won't be the last time I say it today," Nice said trying to engage her.

"I saw you reading in there. What were you looking up?"

"I was wondering about something." Nice replied trying to minimize her interest in his mission.

"Those books are antiques. You're not going to find anything useful in there."

"Do you know a lot about science?" Nice asked wondering if Chelbi may be a resource.

"No. Can't stand it," she bluntly retorted.

"Guys, it's time to eat," Ben called out through the sliding glass door.

Nice bent down to pick up Yappy, who eagerly entered his arms.

"What's your dog's name?" Chelbi inquired, but not showing any interest.

"My sister's name is Yappy."

A smirk came over Chelbi.

"Your sister, huh? Does everyone in your family have an odd name?"

"A name is just a tag. It's your heart condition that defines you. *Chelbi*," Nice responded emphasizing her name.

His comment slightly stunned her as she stood from the table and walked directly inside. Yappy was now standing in Nice's arm and licking him on the cheek.

Nice would not be embarrassed by his name, his family, or his devotion to his faith. He was also not deterred by his lack of progress regarding his mission. He would begin tomorrow with a new plan of action.

CHAPTER 7

In a back office of the now-closed Semany Wholesale Flowers, two men spent this Easter day preparing for their evening activity. One man was in his early 40s, 5 feet 6 inches tall and weighed 160 pounds. He wore a light blue Ralph Lauren Polo shirt with blue piping and black Dockers slacks. His name was Tama and he was from Croatia.

The other man who towered over Tama was Molech, wearing the same jeans he wore the day before, in addition to a black hoodie that zipped up the front, his black, curly hair wig, and eye patch. They were both standing as their conversation progressed.

"When are you going to hear from the rest of your people?" Molech inquired.

"Shortly. We have all the targets under surveillance. We'll take the easiest one first," Tama told him.

As Tama spoke, Molech walked over to a locked medical waste disposal container that hung on the wall. It was approximately eighteen inches wide, twelve inches high, and six inches deep. Molech unlocked the container, then proceeded to put on a pair of disposable latex gloves that he pulled out of a box on a nearby bookshelf. Molech reached into the disposable container and pulled out a glass vial.

"You think you should be doing that?" Tama asked.

"It's for our friends in law enforcement, in case they want to get nosey. It's the last place they want to look," Molech responded with devious pride.

From a lower shelf, Molech retrieved a plastic case and set it on the desk. He wiped the vial with a nearby cloth, took off the gloves and disposed of them in the same disposal container. Molech then opened the plastic case and set within a preformed foam insert was a jet injector vaccine gun. Molech removed it from its case and inserted a carbon dioxide gas cartridge into the handle like the magazine of a pistol. He then took the vial that he removed from the disposal container and attached it, upside down, to the top of the device through what appeared to be a hypodermic needle.

This process would deliver the injection liquid through a high pressure narrow jet to penetrate the skin. The process was considered very efficient.

The vial contained vecuronium bromide. This is a muscle relaxant that is utilized with general anesthesia prior to surgery. Even though it is considered by some to be a muscle relaxant, it is more accurately classified as a paralyzing agent.

"What does she weigh?" Molech quizzed Tama quickly demanding a response as he manipulated the device.

"Who?"

"The first one."

Tama opened a folder on the desk and ran his finger down a page.

"The driver's license says one-ten," Tama responded indicating that the person weighed 110 pounds. "Why do you need to know that?"

"To calibrate the dose."

"Why do you think he wants them?" Tama asked rhetorically.

"Don't know. Don't care. It's none of my business." Molech answered succinctly.

"They say he's from Ireland."

"Who?" Molech asked continuing to calibrate the device.

"Feardesin." Tama responded looking out a barred window of the office without focus. Feardesin was the man who hired Molech. "Are you religious?"

"Nope.

"Me neither."

"That stuff is all voodoo and hocus-pocus to me," Molech added.

Then Tama augmented his comment, insightfully, "I've never met him, but whenever I talk to Feardesin on the phone, I wish I was religious."

CHAPTER 8

As the late afternoon turned into the early evening, Sally and Theresa had just finished cleaning the kitchen when two sets of guests arrived for coffee and a piece of cake.

Ben had returned to his favorite chair in front of the television watching the local news and Chelbi had returned to her chair on the patio. Yappy had received a new Dalmatian squeak toy from Ben, so Yappy would encourage Nice to throw it and Nice gladly obliged.

The first visitors to arrive were Bob and Betty Rondolay. They were originally from Georgia and had been married for the past fifty-one years. Bob was 72 years old, 5 feet 9 inches tall, 185 pounds with a full head of hair that was colored black. He wore a yellow sweater, a white golf shirt, and gray slacks.

Betty Rondolay was 71 years old, 5 feet 5 inches tall, also 185 pounds with a blonde bouffant hairdo. She considered herself a 'Georgia Peach,' complete with an accent and a lexicon that sounded like she just walked off the set of *Gone with the Wind*.

Betty wore a short sleeve, black button shirt, black pants, and a red sweater. She had a gold necklace and three rings on one hand

and two rings on the other. Betty was always smiling and full of energy. The Rondolays brought a pecan pie with them for the group.

The other visitors to arrive were Wayne and Marion Patterson. They were just returning from visiting their cancer-stricken daughter, who was being treated for *glioblastoma mulitforme*, the deadliest form of inoperable brain cancer, at the Palomar Medical Center in Escondido, California.

Ben was delighted to see all the guests and invited them to sit at the dining room table.

"Everybody have a good Easter?" Ben asked the crowd as Theresa and Sally joined the visitors at the dining room table.

A rousing chorus of "Yes" filled the air.

"Nice," Sally called to him in a rather petulant tone. "Where are your manners? Get over here."

Nice sprung up from the floor and entered the dining room.

"Peace be with everyone," Nice shared with the crowd, then found a seat at the table.

From where he sat at the end of the table, Ben called out through the sliding glass door.

"Chelbi, come and meet our friends."

Chelbi came in from outside and entered the dining room. She stood behind an empty chair, but did not sit. Ben went around the table introducing Chelbi to everyone and Betty Rondolay took the opportunity to say more than just 'Hello.'

"You are the cutest little baby doll," Betty told her, then turned to Ben. "This your son's daughter?"

"No. My daughter, Shelly's daughter."

"How old are you, honey?" Betty asked with her southern twang.

"Twenty-two," Chelbi responded nonchalantly.

"Twenty-two! Tarnation. I wouldn't think you were twixt twelve and twenty." Betty did not think she appeared old enough to be a teenager. "I'll tell you what, cutie pie. You and I gonna have to go for breakfast one-a these days to get acquainted. I'm the treasurer of the Woman's Auxiliary down at church. We're always lookin' for ways to raise money. And we could use some young blood. Oh, and I'm also good with makeup."

"Okay," Chelbi answered apathetically.

"Just to help you remember, it's Betty and Bob," she said first pointing to herself, then her husband. "B and B."

"Betty was once in the Miss Georgia Peach Contest," Bob piped in proudly. "She was always a real looker."

"Chelbi, welcome to Carlsbad," Wayne declared with a forced smile. His mind was still in the hospital room with his daughter.

"Wasn't the weather beautiful today?" Theresa asked to redirect the conversation.

"It sure was. I heard they got freezing rain in Georgia," Betty relayed.

"What's the name of that priest that comes once a year when Father Tom goes on vacation?" Ben inquired of the group.

"Father Ray," Wayne's wife, Marion, was quick to respond.

"That's right," Ben acknowledged as if it just came to him. "And his last name was a car name."

"Fairmont," Nice responded immediately.

"That's it, Father Ray Fairmont," Ben agreed. "I remember he said once that Carlsbad is the place where God goes on vacation. What do you think?"

"Don't get me started on it," Wayne responded forcefully. "Because if you run into God, I'd like to ask him a few questions. Like how does my daughter go from absolutely normal one day, then twenty-four hours later, she's bedridden with an inoperable brain tumor? As Father Tom would like to say to God, 'No wonder you have so many enemies, look at the way you treat your friends.'"

"To be honest, Father Tom didn't say that, Saint Teresa of Avila in Spain did," Sally said, adding her voice to the mix.

"I don't want to talk about it," Wayne stated conclusively.

"How many people want decaf?" Theresa asked as she tallied the amount for a coffee order.

Ben turned to Wayne for a more private conversation, who was sitting adjacent to him at the end of the table.

"You need to redirect your anger, my friend. Save it for the man of sin, Satan. He's the one who brings evil into this world."

Wayne looked at Ben without comment.

"I don't know, Ben," Wayne rubbed his forehead as he spoke. "I feel like I've said more prayers than there are stars in the sky, but I don't think anybody is listening."

"It's going to be all right, my friend. I'm telling you."

Ben's assurance had no impact on Wayne. All he wanted to do now was finish his coffee and cake and return to the hospital.

CHAPTER 9

It was night. Sheila Delucia lived in a first floor apartment located on Tamarack Avenue, near Skyline Road. The apartments were approximately forty years old, but well maintained, both for the landscape and the buildings.

Sheila was twenty-four years old, 5 feet 2 inches tall and 113 pounds. She worked in the shoe department of a Macy's store located in the Plaza Camino Real Mall, less than two miles from where she lived.

Sheila wore a t-shirt from Occidental College and striped boxer shorts.

At 2:20 am, in her darkened bedroom, Sheila was in a deep, REM sleep, dreaming about the time her family took a trip in their Oldsmobile Vista Cruiser station wagon to Disneyland. In the dream, Sheila's father drove and Sheila's mother was directing Sheila's two brothers and two sisters to sing travel songs. As she slept on her left side, a smile could be seen on her face.

Back in reality, her slumber was being watched from the end of her bed by Mr. Molech, with his jet injector vaccine gun in hand loaded with vecuronium bromide. He watched her without an expression on his face and waited for two other men to enter the room. He nodded his head affirmatively to both of them.

The men proceeded to each side of the bed and Molech followed the man on the left side of the bed. The man on the right side of the bed pinned down her left arm at the wrist and covered her mouth with his other hand. At the same time, the other man grabbed her right wrist and pulled it over to pin her down, so she would lie flat on her back.

Sheila awoke as soon as she was touched and fought mightily to free one of her hands. She saw Molech's jet injector vaccine gun coming at her neck. For a moment, she freed her right hand, swatting the gun once and then swatting at Molech's face. Part of one of her fingernails caught his eye patch and flipped it up. In the moonlight, the horror of his visage paralyzed her for a moment in fear. As she trembled, with a frozen gaze on his milky cornea, Molech took the opportunity to inject her directly into her carotid artery.

In less than sixty seconds, Sheila stopped moving and the men let her go. Molech looked at the man who lost his grip on her.

"You have one thing to do and you can't do it?" Molech asked as he stared at him and flipped down his eye patch. "If it happens again, I'll cut your arm off. Because it's useless."

At this point, three other men had entered the apartment. Molech gave one final series of orders.

"Find the cars keys, get her purse, get some clothes and a suitcase if you can find one. Then get the mail, clear the answering machine, and shut it off. Last thing, get the perishable food out of the refrigerator."

The men all moved stealthily to fulfill his commands.

In the few seconds after Sheila was injected, but before she passed out, she wondered if perhaps her dream simply had a perverse twist to it. Maybe, she would wake up in the morning and it would all be just a bad dream.

But when Sheila did wake up, her nightmare was about to begin.

CHAPTER 10

At 9:45 am on this Monday, the four employees of Ben's Glassworks assembled to discuss the day's itinerary. In addition to Ben and Nice, there was Lozo, whose name was Lorenzo Estrada. He was Hispanic, thirty-six years old, 5 feet 8 inches tall and 190 pounds. His hair was extremely close-cropped, almost bald, and he had a black goatee. He had worked for Ben for the past sixteen years. He was married and had four children, between the ages of three to fifteen years.

The other employee was Diz. His name was Dennis Halstrom. He was African-American, sixty-one years old, 5 feet 7 inches tall and 170 pounds. His hair was black and wavy, and he occasionally smoked a pipe. The type of pipe he smoked was referred to as a half bent Dublin, the same kind of pipe that Sherlock Holmes would have smoked. He had worked for Ben for thirty-nine years, three months less than the entire time Ben's Glassworks was open.

Nice and Lozo wore Ben's Glassworks t-shirts that were light blue with a large logo on the back and a smaller logo over a breast pocket. They both wore Dickies dark blue uniform pants.

Diz wore a navy-colored, Dickies flame resistant light coverall, with the shop's logo on the back. He also wore an extremely weathered, Chicago Cubs baseball cap.

Ben's Glassworks was located in an industrial strip center on a street called Avenida Encinas, near a set of railroad tracks and within a half-mile from the Pacific Ocean. It was essentially a large, garage stall with white walls, and an overhead door, wide enough for three cars that covered one wall. It also included a fabrication area and a glass cutting area. There was a counter for customers and a small office for Ben. Outside of his office was an area for a coffee maker and a refrigerator.

Ben put on his reading glasses and skimmed a clipboard of jobs in progress that were printed up each day by his wife.

"Lozo, what's going on with the Geisserelli job?" Ben asked as he commenced the work day.

"That's the one where the neighbor got the restraining order and the work stopped on Thursday. You're gonna attend the subcontractor's meeting, right?" Lozo inquired of Ben.

"Oh, yeah," he then recalled. "I can attend by phone. What about your day worker buddies? I hate to lose them."

"It shouldn't be a problem. We've got enough work to keep them busy."

"All right. The bay window came in for the Garubowitz house," Ben advised as he pointed to a large box with straps on it, eight feet long, five feet high, and three feet wide.

"I had my guys build a support wall under the ceiling joists on Friday," Lozo told him.

"Be sure the power's off before you start tearing apart the wall," Ben reminded him.

"I got it, Benny," Lozo reassured him. "Can Nice come with me? I trust him to operate the come-along."

Lozo was referring to a hand operated ratchet lever winch. This is a mechanical device, used with a rope or cable that allows heavy objects to be lifted with greater ease. The device has a mechanical brake that keeps the rope or cable from unwinding. The come-along winch would be connected to an extending arm that swivels from the back of their truck and allows them to lift and position the bay window into place.

"That's a good idea," Ben concurred. "Diz, you in the shop today?"

"All day, except I wanted Nice to take some measurements on a commercial building over on Salk Avenue. It's only two broken windows."

"I can get that done today," Nice responded.

"It shouldn't take us more than a couple of hours," Lozo said.

"Okay," Ben relayed with a smile. "Let's start the day."

Lozo went outside to back their truck up to the garage door and Nice grabbed the come-along off one of the tool shelves.

"Hey Nice," Ben called over to get his attention. "If you guys are going out to eat, call me. Okay?"

"Sure. Listen Ben, can I use the computer after work?"

"No problem. Make sure your mother knows where you are," Ben recommended. "Hey, I taped *The Searchers*. You know, John Wayne. You want to come over tonight and watch it?"

"Count me in," Nice answered trying to mimic Ben's enthusiasm.

"Come on over when you're done here. Theresa will whip somethin' up for both of us."

"I'll be there," Nice assured him.

"Grab a water for you and Lozo," Ben told him pointing with his thumb to the refrigerator.

Nice grabbed two water bottles and his black, lunch cooler. Inside the lunch cooler was a bag lunch prepared by his mother and his Bible. This day was beginning as any other day would begin. The difference was that Nice's fortunes were about to change.

CHAPTER 11

Theresa Krische, Ben's wife, always began the week with dusting followed by a workout with the vacuum. She had a slight concern this day because she did not know when Chelbi would wake up. She decided to stick to her regular routine and Chelbi would have to adjust if she didn't like it.

She retrieved a pile of dust cloths from under the sink in her laundry room and a can of Endust when the ring of the telephone shattered her silence. Theresa moved quickly to the phone that hung on the kitchen wall by the doorway entrance.

"Hello," Theresa answered.

"Hi, Theresa. It's Betty." The voice on the other end of the phone was Betty Rondolay, one of the visitors for coffee and cake the night before.

"Hi, Betty. How are you today?" Theresa was definitely pleased to hear her voice.

"I'm just fine," Betty answered with a pumped up voice. "Where's that little June bug granddaughter of yours? I want to invite her to breakfast."

"She's not up yet. I haven't seen her. Would you like me to wake her?"

"Yes, please. And Theresa, mention to her that if she doesn't talk to me now, I'll come over there and talk to her."

"Okay, hold on," Theresa politely told her.

Betty was used to getting her way and she was of the belief that Chelbi needed a little 'tough' love.

When Theresa reached Chelbi's bedroom door, she knocked, but there was no answer. Theresa slowly opened the door and saw Chelbi lying on top of the unmade bed looking at the ceiling, dressed in a t-shirt and jeans, wearing earbuds connected to an iPod with music blaring.

Theresa walked up to her to get her attention. When she saw Theresa, Chelbi was slightly startled. She quickly sat up and pulled the earbuds out of her ears.

"Yes, grandma?" she asked.

"You have a phone call," Theresa told her and pointed to a pink, Princess phone on the night table next to the bed.

"Okay. Thanks," Chelbi said as Theresa did an about-face for a quick exit out of the room.

"Hello," Chelbi said as she wondered who was calling.

"Chelbi? It's Betty Rondolay. You remember, from last night?"

"Oh, hi," Chelbi responded with a less than enthusiastic salutation.

"I was thinking. You're new to town. We gotta get together and do a little girl talk. I can give ya the lay of the land. What do you say? Tomorrow. Breakfast?" Betty spoke so fast it would be impossible to interrupt her.

"Oh, I don't know," Chelbi whined.

"Honey. Honey. Honey," Betty retorted as if she was calming Chelbi down. "While you're trying to make up your mind, another girl's gonna swoop in and get your man! You don't want that. You gotta know what you want, take it, and hold on to it. You can't stay in the middle of the road, because eventually you're gonna get hit by a car. I've been on the bus a long time and I know where all the stops are. You listen to Betty and I'll make y'all the belle of the ball."

Chelbi's head was slightly spinning trying to process everything Betty said.

"Okay," Chelbi relented. "What time?"

"Let's see. Will you be in church tomorrow morning?"

"No."

"All right, then. I'll come and pick you up at 9:45." There was a slight pause. "You know, let's make it ten o'clock. Tomorrow's donut day at church. Sometimes you get gabbin' and you lose track of the time."

"Okay," Chelbi acknowledged in a meek voice, "I'll be ready."

"See you tomorrow, sweetie."

With that, the call ended. As Chelbi was returning the phone to its cradle, she thought that her visit with Betty would be an epic waste of time. What Chelbi didn't know was that she was on a collision course with a runaway freight train, loaded with Mack trucks, named Betty Rondolay.

CHAPTER 12

By early afternoon, Lozo and Nice had finished their installation of the Bay window at the Garubowitz house and they were heading back to the shop. Nice was perusing his Bible, reviewing random passages, without much detail. Suddenly, he decided to switch focus and use the opportunity for a conversation.

"Lozo, you good with science?" Nice wondered.

"I'm not the guy for that," Lozo acknowledged. "You know who you should talk to? Diz."

"Yeah," Nice answered with surprise.

"Diz is real smart. He's got a Master's Degree in petrochemical engineering."

"So, he's probably like a scientist, huh?" Nice presumed. "What does that kind of scientist study?"

"You know, I'm not really sure. It's got something to do with crude oil, natural gas, gasoline. Stuff like that."

Nice absorbed the information that Lozo was sharing, but he did not think it would help him find a time machine. After a moment, Nice decided on another line of questioning.

"Do you ever shoot guns?" Nice inquired.

"I've done it before. Is it something you'd like to do? We can go to the range sometime."

"Do you know where I could buy a gun?"

"What do you need a gun for?" Lozo's question did not imply shock, but rather concern.

"I was just thinking about buying one."

"You got trouble with somebody?" Lozo wanted to know. "You tell me, I'll handle it."

"No. It's nothing like that. It's just something I was interested in."

"You don't want a gun." Lozo was conclusive. "They're trouble."

Nice decided that Lozo would not be a good resource for the machine gun portion of his plan.

About three miles down the street from the house they just left, Lozo spied a Ford F650 flatbed, in the parking lot of a grocery store, loading a late model Acura onto the truck. Lozo pulled into the next entrance to the parking lot and slowed down as he pulled up alongside of the wrecker. On the door of the flatbed, in block letters, were the words, 'COLLISION LOGISTICS.'

"Roll down your window," he told Nice. "I want to talk to this guy."

The driver of the flatbed recognized Lozo and walked over to Nice's window with a big smile. He was in his early 30s, 5 feet 8 inches tall, 200 pounds, and wore black coveralls with a Collision Logistics logo on the back.

"Hey, *esé*," said the wrecker truck driver, with an ear-to-ear smile as he approached the Ben's Glassworks truck.

"What are you doin'?" Lozo asked, with a similar big smile. "You should be stealing better cars."

Nice was nervous about Lozo's comment.

"I think the engine seized up on this one, but I don't want to tell the owner. You keeping busy?"

"Yeah. This is a friend of mine. Nice," Lozo informed the driver. "Nice, this is Carlos."

"Hey, nice to meet ya." They shared a quick handshake.

"Same here. Peace be with you."

"You got anything good?" Lozo interjected.

"What do you need? You know me. If I don't got it, I can get it. You need some rims? I got some smoking, cool twenty-twos." Carlos was referring to twenty-two inch custom car rims.

"I don't need any rims," Lozo advised.

"If you need anything, let me know."

"I will," Lozo answered with a smile.

"Hey, my kids broke a window on one of my screen doors. What's that gonna cost to fix?" Carlos queried.

"It's Plexiglas, right?"

"Yeah."

"Drop the frame off at the shop. Tell Benny it's for me and not to write a ticket for it."

"So, what's it going to cost?"

"Usually, a case of beer. But for you, a six-pack."

Carlos smiled and Nice was enjoying their banter.

"Do you want Dos Equis or Pacifico?" Carlos asked.

"Surprise me."

"Hey, I gotta bounce," Carlos conveyed. "Nice to meet you . . . Nice?"

"You got it," Nice assured him. "Same here."

"Later, Gee," Lozo added to conclude the conversation.

A comment made by Carlos had Nice thinking. As he and Lozo drove off, Nice had a few questions.

"What does it mean when you said, 'Later, Gee?'"

"The 'Gee' stands for gangster. It's like a term of respect."

"What does it mean when he says he's got to bounce?"

"That just means he's got to get going someplace."

"When he first came over to the truck, he called you the letters 'S – A'?"

"No, he said '*esé.*' That's Spanish. It's just like saying the word, 'guy.'"

"Where did you meet him?" Nice wondered.

"It must have been twenty years ago in the county lockup."

Nice knew that Lozo had a criminal past and he never pushed him for details. He paid his debt to society and Ben trusted him. That's all Nice needed to know.

Nice was appreciative that Lozo was like Ben. He never was upset with anything Nice did and he was a good teacher.

"Lozo, do you think I'm a weirdo? I mean, there is so much I don't know."

"Nice, you are the most normal guy I know or have ever known. I would like a guy like you to marry one of my daughters."

Lozo had two daughters both under the age of eight years old. His comment brought a smile to Nice's face.

"Let's go get something to eat," Nice suggested. "I'll call Ben."

Looking back on the day's events, Nice was pleased that he may have found a machine gun vendor.

CHAPTER 13

Detective Wayne Patterson and his partner, Andy Sandoval, had just completed talking with a witness to a crime involving an Automated Teller Machine 'smash and grab' at a nearby shopping center in downtown Carlsbad. They were riding in an unmarked, late-model Chevrolet Caprice and Detective Sandoval was driving.

Wayne wore a charcoal blazer with a white shirt and a black diamond patterned tie. Andy wore a dark olive sport coat, with a light blue shirt, and a red, paisley-patterned tie.

"We didn't get much out of that guy," Andy admitted conclusively.

"It's the same guys who did it in Oceanside, Vista, and San Marcos," Wayne told him like a wise, old sage. The cities that he referenced were all adjacent to Carlsbad. "Oceanside PD told me they know who it is. They're just waiting for them to slip up. All they need to do is get a print off the ATMs or the vehicles they steal for the smash. When we get back, call the crime lab and ask them to make it a priority."

"Where do you want to go for lunch?" Andy asked.

"Anywhere," Wayne responded, without giving it much thought. As they cruised down Grand Avenue, about a block ahead,

Wayne saw what appeared to be a homeless man trying to flag them down. "Hey, let's stop and talk to this guy."

"This is your buddy, right?" Andy chimed in.

"He's given us some good intel in the past."

The car stopped along the curbside and Wayne rolled down his window. The homeless man, who appeared tired, was the first to speak.

"Hey, Detective Wayne, Happy Easter."

"Happy Easter, Zeke. What have you been up to?"

Zeke was thirty-eight years old, but he looked more like sixty-eight. He was 5 feet 9 inches tall, 165 pounds with hair that was so dirty, it looked like it was combed back with grease. He had a beard that looked like a Brillo pad extending six inches from his face and his t-shirt and pants were so dirty and tattered, it was impossible to distinguish their original color.

Not far from where Zeke stood was a grocery cart filled with all of his worldly possessions.

"Just trying to get through the day," Zeke replied with a smile, showing that he was missing several teeth on the top and bottom of his mouth.

"What do you hear on the street?" Wayne quizzed.

Zeke looked up and down Grand Avenue, then pulled his face closer to the car window. His body odor and bad breath were noticeable in the car.

"A group of guys were planning to jack these three girls. All locals. I heard they already got one of 'em."

Wayne was now very interested.

"What for? Kidnapping? Sex trade?"

"Don't know. The guy who set it up is from outta town and real mysterious."

"You got any names?"

"The local guy running it is named Molech. I don't know how to spell it. They're supposed to grab the other two girls this week." Zeke looked at Wayne. "That's all I know. So, could you help out an old altar boy?"

Wayne reached for his wallet as he started to speak.

"If you hear anything else, you stop one of the patrol cars and tell them to call me. I'll tell the patrol officers in this area to keep an eye out for you."

As Wayne finished his sentence, he removed a twenty dollar bill. Wayne folded it and handed it to Zeke between two fingers.

"Thanks, friend," Zeke told him as he patted the window sill of the car door and backed a step away.

"No liquor. No drugs. Right?" Wayne shared an admonition.

"Not today," Zeke answered, pointing his finger at Wayne. "Maybe tomorrow."

"Take it easy," Wayne conveyed as the police car pulled away from the curb.

Wayne watched Zeke in the side mirror of his door and for some reason the writing at the bottom of the mirror caught his eye: 'OBJECTS IN MIRROR ARE CLOSER THAN THEY APPEAR.'

CHAPTER 14

About a mile and a half north of Ben's Glassworks was a strip shopping center called Poinsettia Village. The center had an eclectic collection of stores and included a freestanding Jack-in the-Box restaurant at the northern end.

Nice and Lozo proceeded to the Jack-in-the-Box after Nice spoke to Ben to get a lunch order. Ben told Nice that he and Diz both wanted a Jumbo Jack with fries and a drink. Ben wanted an Oreo milkshake for his drink.

Even though Lozo and Diz had worked for Ben longer, Ben gave a company credit card to Nice. Nice's mother, Sally, would have never entertained the thought of Nice applying for a credit card, but Ben had faith in him. It also made it easier to send Nice to pick up various items for the shop.

Whenever all four men were in the shop at lunchtime, Ben would treat them all to fast food lunch. On the other days, if Nice was around, he would send him on a 'food run' for lunch. Ben considered it a cheap company perk.

Ben also allowed Nice to take a company pickup truck home every night. Nice could use it for personal reasons because, once again, he wanted to prove that Nice was able to handle the responsibility of having a vehicle. In addition, as Ben became older, he was not fond of driving. Neither was Diz. But Nice was always ready to run an errand when requested.

At the drive-through window, the Jack-in-the-Box employee handed the food order to Lozo, who handed it to Nice. As they began to proceed forward, Lozo slowed down.

"Hey, check the order to make sure they gave us everything," Lozo directed.

Nice quickly looked through the bag.

"It's all here."

Their truck turned onto the exit/entrance way at the northern end of the shopping center. Located approximately one hundred feet ahead, at the corner of the exit and Avenida Encinas, stood a homeless man, 5 feet 11 inches tall, 170 pounds, in his early 30s, with longer, curly, brown hair, beard and moustache. He had a rather nice complexion for a homeless man and his green eyes were mesmerizing. He wore a double-breasted, blue pea coat that was worn from dirt and age. His slacks were a military green that were worn to the thread at the bottom of each leg. On his feet, he wore simple sandals.

The homeless man held a weathered, handwritten sign that said, in block letters, 'ANYTHING WILL HELP.'

Nice spied the man as their truck approached him to turn onto Avenida Encinas. As they neared him, Nice unzipped his lunch cooler and took out the bag lunch prepared by his mother.

"Stop a second," he told Lozo as they reached the corner.

Nice rolled down his window and held the bag lunch out to the man. He stepped up to the truck as if he had just won a prize.

"My mother made it. I'm not gonna eat it," Nice shared with him.

"Thank you," was his genuine reply.

"Here." Nice then handed him one of the sodas that they just bought. "I got a water."

"Thank you so much," the homeless man answered with a smile.

"Peace be with you," Nice responded with his usual salutation.

The homeless man said something to Nice, but he couldn't hear it over the engine of the truck revving up to turn onto the road.

"You know," Lozo began, "I saw this thing on TV that said a lot of homeless people aren't really homeless. They come from other counties to places where people don't know them, so they can play on people's sympathies."

"I don't know, Lozo. You gotta do what's right," Nice answered with certainty. "You know what Ben says?"

Lozo gazed forward without focus. Then he replied.

"What's right is right."

CHAPTER 15

It was approximately 8:00 pm when Nice and Ben finished a late night dinner at Ben's house. Nice had spent approximately two hours at the end of day researching time travel, but his research did not bear fruit. Most of the information dealing with time travel and time machines concerned fictional accounts and the information that dealt with the science behind time travel was just too complicated for him to comprehend. Nice decided that he needed help.

This evening was to be devoted to John Wayne and *The Searchers*. Nice had seen the movie with Ben at least four times before, but was always ready to see it again if Ben asked him. Ben took a seat on his favorite Barcalounger and Nice was comfortable sitting on the couch.

"Would you boys like dessert?" Theresa inquired.

"Yes," Ben quickly replied without missing a beat.

"Okay," Theresa followed up, "I've got pumpkin cheesecake and pecan pie."

"What do you say, Nice?" Ben asked.

Nice wasn't really in the mood for dessert, but he would always ask for a piece and Ben would finish it for him.

"I'll try the pecan pie," Nice responded.

"Would you like whipped cream on it?" Theresa asked.

"Sure."

As Ben was cueing up the movie, the telephone rang. Theresa answered it and then brought a cordless phone to Ben.

"It's Gordy from the Double Daily."

Ben looked at her as if he was wondering why he would be calling. The Double Dailey was a small dive bar located in downtown Carlsbad. To most people driving by, it was not noticeable. It catered to the older, military clientele. Ben and Gordy's father were both in the Knights of Columbus at St. Elizabeth Seton Church.

"Hello," Ben answered.

"Hey, Ben. How are ya?" Gordy responded, speaking quickly. "Listen, there's a young girl down here. She doesn't even look like she's a teenager with a Kansas ID saying she's twenty-two. She says she's your granddaughter. Should I serve her?"

"No," Ben stated with certainty. "I'll be right down there."

Nice could see that the phone call changed Ben's mood and he was struggling to get out of the chair.

"Ben, what's wrong?" Nice posed his inquiry.

"It's Chelbi. Where did she say she was going?" he asked, directing his question to Theresa.

"To the mall with her friend, Tracy."

"Well, she's down at the Double Daily trying to order drinks. I'm going to go and get her."

"Let me go get her," Nice offered. "I can be there and back, real quick."

Ben truly appreciated the offer.

"You sure?"

"Yeah, it's no problem," Nice assured him. "I know Gordy."

"Okay," Ben told him. "Bring her back. She shouldn't be drinking."

Nice got up off the couch and headed to the door.

"Call me if there's a problem," Ben told him as he exited the house.

Within ten minutes, Nice was parking in front of the Double Dailey, located on State Street in downtown Carlsbad. Foot traffic on the street had died down considerably at this time of night. Nice made a beeline to the front door of the bar and entered.

The Double Dailey consisted of a bar with stools that allowed twelve people to sit. Everything had a dark, maple veneer and was aged from a half century earlier. It also contained six circular tables that allowed four patrons per table and there was a ledge around the perimeter that allowed people to set their drinks while they stood and talked.

Once inside, Nice took a quick visual scan of the interior and spotted Chelbi, sitting on a bar stool, surrounded by five young Marines, all dressed in civilian clothes. She was the only female in the bar and there was one other regular patron at the opposite end of the bar. Gordy, the bartender, noticed Nice.

"Hey, Nice."

Gordy was 5 feet 8 inches tall, 220 pounds, balding with black hair and a moustache. He was wearing a black sweatshirt.

"Hi, Gordy. Peace be with you." As Nice spoke to Gordy, he approached Chelbi. She did not notice him. When Nice was within two feet of her, he began to speak.

"Chelbi, let's go," Nice told her.

She turned and was surprised to see him, still dressed in his blue Ben's Glassworks t-shirt.

"I'm not going with you, Lieutenant Buzzkill," Chelbi told him and turned back to ignore him and speak with her marine friends.

"Yes, you are," Nice announced without emotion and dead serious calm.

"You should mind your own business," the tallest Marine said to him.

"She is my business," Nice stated and stared him in the eyes shifting his glance to the other men to see what action they may, or may not take.

In addition to teaching Nice a trade involving glass, Ben also taught him how to fight. Especially, in scenarios where he was outnumbered. In his hand was a key ring and he positioned the keys, one between each finger, to act as a type of brass knuckles, if necessary.

In the moment when he was awaiting some type of physical confrontation, he could hear the words of his pastor, Father Tom Hayes, at perhaps the worst possible moment.

Think before you speak or act. When provoked, do not retaliate. If anger wells up, take your leave.

It was then that Gordy spoke up. He had a bat in his hand and rapped it on top of the bar.

"I'm cutting you off," he said pointing to Chelbi. "I can't verify this Kansas license, so I'm not taking any chances. Everybody else, if you want to try something, I'm gonna take batting practice then call the cops."

Everyone stared at each other for a moment.

"You," Gordy declared, again pointing to Chelbi. "Get out. Go with him," pointing to Nice. "NOW!"

Nice went to grab her arm and she violently shook it loose.

"You want to treat me like a baby," she informed Nice. "Then you can carry me out of here like a baby."

Chelbi threw her arms around Nice's neck, which she could barely reach, jumped up and straddled his right side. He put his right forearm under her butt for support. He turned to leave the bar and Chelbi told him, "Don't talk to me."

Nothing was said during the car ride back to Ben's house. Nice escorted Chelbi to the door and Theresa answered it.

"Hi, Theresa," Nice said speaking through a screen door. Chelbi briskly walked inside in a huff without acknowledging her grandmother.

"Thank you, Nice," Theresa expressed with gratitude.

"It's no big deal. Tell Ben that we'll catch that movie tomorrow and I'll see him in the morning."

Nice returned to his truck to head home.

Chelbi went directly to her room to sulk. She put the earbuds to her iPod in her ears and began playing music in an attempt to drown out any other sounds. She thought about the confrontation in the bar and one sentence in particular that she enjoyed kept playing in her mind over and over. It was Nice saying, "She is my business."

CHAPTER 16

The Beach Plum Restaurant had a reputation for comfortable dining and putting a healthy spin on simple classic meals. The name of the restaurant is derived from a coastal fruit that grows in the wild from Maine to Virginia. This particular fruit is surrounded in mystery because its supply, in any one year, is unpredictable.

The interior of the restaurant was open and airy, consisting of booths and tables. There was also a counter for the solo visitor and a staff that was always in motion.

Betty Rondolay and Chelbi Gorringe were seated immediately in a booth next to the glass wall in the front of the restaurant.

Betty wore a Lane Bryant printed woven cardigan, a white, embellished high-low blouse, and black, Ashley cotton smart stretch leg pants.

Chelbi wore a purple t-shirt with the words, BIG THINGS COME IN LITTLE PACKAGES, an oversized flannel shirt with a pattern of skulls, and machine black distressed wash skinny jeans. Her shoes were T.U.K. black quilted Viva Mondo Creepers on a raised platform.

They gave their drink order to the waitress and there was an uncomfortable silence.

"This place is really popular with the church crowd," Betty began. "You should try the lemon re-cot-a buttermilk pancakes. Oh, to die for."

Chelbi smiled and wondered what she was doing there.

"Where do you buy your clothes, honey?" Betty wondered.

"Mostly Hot Topic."

"Hot Topic?" Betty responded with shocked aplomb. "Isn't that the place in the mall, real dark inside, looks like they're sacrificing babies in the back?"

The comment brought a smile to Chelbi's face.

"That's not where a refined young lady buys her clothes," Betty advised with serious candor.

"Maybe I should buy my clothes where you buy yours," Chelbi replied with a bit of attitude.

"You know I come from down in the South, where a young'un respects their elders and when they don't, why it's not outta line for an elder to give that young'un a slap from outta nowhere, like a lightning bolt. Now, you wouldn't want me to do that, would ya, honey bun?" Betty's smile masked a sincere threat.

"No," Chelbi relented.

"Now, I want us to be friends," Betty announced. "A good friend gives good advice. Somebody as cute as you should not be wearing clothes that make you look like a hobo that's been ridin' the rails. You want attention, then your personality, grace, and charm will get it for you. Don't depend on a shirt that looks like it came from Goodwill. Don't think you're gonna find it in a bar surrounded by a bunch of drunk horndogs."

"What is there a hotline in this town for gossip? Or is there a need to tell each other every time you take a piss or a dump?" Chelbi fumed. "Big deal. I like a beer every once in a while."

"Now, there you go using language that is unbecoming of a little cutie pie. First of all, beer is swill for pigs. Second of all, if you don't like that people care about you, then tough. But we're a family and family takes care of one another."

Betty and Chelbi gazed at each other, then Chelbi looked away. The waitress then appeared at the table.

"Do you need a few more minutes?" the waitress asked.

"We do," Betty responded. "Come back in a few."

"I know why you're here in Carlsbad," Betty spoke in a slow, ominous tone. "I know what happened to you back in Kansas."

"So what?" Chelbi articulated with resentment. "What do you want, a medal?"

"I want you to trust me," Betty articulated.

Chelbi had no comment.

"Do you like Nice?" Betty asked.

"Who?"

"Nice. Nicean. Do you like him?"

"I think he and his family are a bunch of weirdos."

"I wanna tell you a little bit about him. His daddy was a drinker. Not a social drinker. He liked to drink until he was, as we say in the South, 'lit.' Nice wasn't even a year old and his daddy went on a binge one night. He was lit. He put Nice in a car seat, but didn't buckle him in. Driving home from the parking lot of a grocery store, he hits a lady head-on. Nice flies out of his seat and hits the front windshield head first. They thought that little baby was gonna die, but the Lord had plans for Nice and he made it through. They told his momma, Sally, that he might be learning disabled. So, she homeschooled him, made him learn Scripture, and kept all the other children and worldly things away from him."

"I didn't think he was learning disabled," Chelbi opined.

"He's not. He's just not worldly. You see out here, all this," Betty told her waving her finger at the parking lot. "This is owned by Satan. This is Satan's world. Nice is not familiar with it. He knows about God's kingdom. He lives his life based on that model. Imagine if everyone did?"

"Are you ready?" the waitress announced.

"Yes," Betty answered without missing a beat. "We'll have two orders of the lemon re-cot-a buttermilk pancakes."

"Very good," the waitress answered and disappeared.

"Now normally, anybody who doesn't know about Satan's world and tried to live in it would be at a severe disadvantage. That's where your grandfather, Ben, comes in. Ben saw what Sally was doing to Nice, so your granddaddy stepped in. Ben and Nice would do sports together. They would lift weights in your grandfather's garage every day and he taught him a trade. Did Nice ever hug you?"

"No," Chelbi answered with a somber tone.

"That boy is like a piece of steel, but as kind as a puppy dog. Nice would not have a driver's license if it wasn't for your grandfather. Ben taught him how to drive and let him have a truck to take home. Your grandfather taught Nice how to be a man and that includes how to treat a lady. If you want to hold it against Nice because he's not worldly, then that says a lot about your character, sugar plum."

"What happened to his father?"

"The grief over the accident took its toll. Shortly after that happened, he went out to the train tracks near Cannon Road and lay down on the tracks just as the Amtrak Surfliner was coming through."

Chelbi thought for a moment about what Betty had said.

"I don't think Nice even knows that story. You think you got a need to tell him, baby doll?"

"No," Chelbi uttered, awed by the revelation.

"Welcome to the family, cupcake," Betty uttered, followed by a wide smile.

"I have never met anyone who talks like you," Chelbi confessed.

"I bet you have. Just this time, you're listening. Now, you got any tattoos?"

Chelbi wondered about the purpose of this question.

"No."

"Good. Because branding is for cattle, not a little dream girl. How 'bout piercings?"

"I had one on the side of my nose, but I stopped wearing it," Chelbi admitted.

Betty took her finger and ran it up and down the side of Chelbi's nose.

"I've got a great concealer for that. I'm gonna turn you into a little Georgia Peach."

"Why are you doing this?"

"We're just two girlfriends jawing," Betty was quick to reply with a big smile. "Now, when we're done eating, we're gonna go to the mall and get you clothes that are fitting for a pretty little thing like you. Then we're gonna go get your hair done. Then a manicure and a pedicure. After that, we're going to my house for a facial and some makeup pointers. Now, if I get any sass or attitude, you remember that lightning bolt slap we talked about?"

Chelbi nodded affirmatively.

"I don't wanna have to put one on ya. All right, girlfriend?" Betty asked and extended her hand to Chelbi to shake.

"You are going to be the belle of the ball. When they see you in church tomorrow, Father Tom's gonna be gettin' chest pains," Betty was already feeling pride in future accomplishments.

"I don't go to church," Chelbi told her, matter-of-factly.

"You do now. You either come with your grandparents or Miss Betty will come over and pour water on your head to wake you up, then I'll dress you and drag you to church by your hair. I'll do it every day until my student learns the routine."

Chelbi just looked at her somewhat shocked, not knowing what to say.

"Satan's gonna fear you," Betty spoke like a politician assuring someone victory. Betty extended her hand to Chelbi.

Chelbi took Betty's hand and agreed. Chelbi was still leery about Betty's intentions, but she had no interest in swimming against the tide. Betty had no interest in opinions, other than her own.

CHAPTER 17

At the Carlsbad Police Headquarters, Wayne Patterson returned the telephone receiver to its cradle while sitting in his cubicle. His mind was continuing to shift focus between his daughter, Joy, who lay helplessly in a hospital bed while cancer ravaged her, and the information provided to him by Zeke, the transient who told him that a girl had been abducted and two more young ladies were on a list.

Wayne wore a short-sleeve, white shirt, a solid blue tie and black pants. His gray sport coat was on the back of his chair. His cubicle was filled with files and reports, but highly organized.

Wayne could find no information in any database regarding a person named Molech. Wayne rested his head on his hand and rubbed his forehead. It was then that his partner, Detective Andy Sandoval, looked at him over his cubicle wall.

"Wayne, Mr. and Mrs. DeLucia are here," Andy told him. "Those are the people I told you about. They filed a missing persons report on their daughter this morning."

"I just got off the phone with the black and white officers we sent over there. Based on the condition of her apartment, it looks like she walked away. They're going to have the crime lab dust for prints."

"You want to talk to them?" Andy asked referring to the DeLucias.

"Sure," Wayne responded as he stood and lifted his sport coat off the chair.

Wayne proceeded down a hallway to a large conference room. Three of the walls were clear glass and a large oak table that was twelve feet long and four feet wide was in the center of the room.

Wayne entered and moved directly to Mr. DeLucia. He was 51 years old, 5 feet 9 inches tall, 210 pounds, clean-shaven, wearing a flowered Hawaiian shirt, green cargo pants, and sandals. Mrs. DeLucia was 49 years old, 5 feet 3 inches tall, 136 pounds with white and gray, close-cropped hair. She wore a denim shirtdress and red elastic ballet flats shoes.

"Mr. and Mrs. DeLucia, I'm Detective Wayne Patterson," Wayne said as he met Mr. DeLucia with a handshake. "I'm so sorry about your inability to contact your daughter."

"We're afraid something has happened," Mr. DeLucia claimed with distress. "She talks to her mother every day. When she didn't call, we knew something happened."

"We sent two patrol officers to her house. No car. Her purse is gone. It looks like clothes have been removed and the refrigerator was quite empty. These are signs of a person who planned to disappear."

"No way," Mrs. DeLucia spoke up with a strident tone. "My daughter loved her life and her family. We have seven children and Sheila was the most sensitive of all my children. She loved going to church and would always volunteer for anything if she was asked."

"Did she have a boyfriend?" Wayne inquired.

"No," Mrs. DeLucia stated. "And no men were bothering her. But I know for sure that she was taken."

"How do you know that?" Wayne's curiosity was piqued.

"Her Bible was still there. She wouldn't leave without it. Our daughter was giving serious consideration to becoming a nun. Her life was the Lord."

Wayne continued to attempt to assuage their concerns, but he recognized that it would have little impact. Wayne realized in his heart that Sheila DeLucia was the first girl abducted. He knew he had to find her and he knew he had to save her.

CHAPTER 18

Nice spent the day 'in the field' traveling to various locations to measure and photograph images of broken glass. He would bring the information back to Ben in the shop, who would write an estimate for repair and contact either the homeowner or business to advise them of the repair cost and see if they wanted the work done.

Nice primarily handled repairs dealing with single pane glass and Plexiglas. He would also assist Lozo and Diz. Lozo handled bigger commercial jobs because he was good at managing day laborers and Diz handled specialty work that was usually delicate. Ben stayed in the shop to coordinate the men and keep them all busy.

Nice finished with his list of repair calls at approximately 2:00 pm. They were all located in the northern section of San Diego County and Nice wanted to make one more stop before returning to the shop.

He pulled in the parking lot of Collision Logistics, located in Vista, California. Vista is situated northeast of Carlsbad and has a reputation for producing a higher rate of gang-related crime.

Collision Logistics was located on Mission Avenue, less than a mile from Rancho Santa Fe Road. It was essentially an old gas station with a yard for their wrecker tow trucks and assorted cars.

This was the company where Lozo's friend, Carlos, was employed. Nice was with Lozo when they spoke with Carlos the day before. At the time, Carlos prided himself on his ability to "get anything."

Nice entered the office and it was old, dirty, and barren with the exception of a gray metal desk in the center of the room. The man sitting behind the desk was 57 years old, 5 feet 8 inches tall, 150 pounds, with white hair and a white beard. He was smoking a cigarette, drinking a Dr. Pepper soda, and reading a car magazine. He wore jeans and a black, long-sleeve t-shirt, with a Corvette logo on the front.

"Can I help you?" he asked while Nice was looking around.

"Is Carlos here?"

"Yeah. Hold on," the man replied. He then yelled into the garage stall area of the building, "Hey, Carlos! Somebody's here to see you."

Within a minute, Carlos emerged from the garage area wearing the same black coveralls he wore the day before.

"Yeah," Carlos said initially directing it to the man at the desk. The man then pointed to Nice.

"Hi, Carlos. Peace be with you. I'm Lozo's friend. From yesterday."

"Oh yeah," he recalled. "I forgot your name?"

"Nice."

"That's right. How could I forget that? How can I help ya?"

Nice looked at him for a moment, not really wanting to talk in front of the man behind the desk.

"Could you come out to my truck?" Nice wondered.

"Sure," Carlos answered. "Lead the way."

Nice walked to the back of his pickup truck and stopped behind the center of the tailgate.

"I got the impression the other day that you're a guy that can get things that are tough to come by?"

"Yeah," Carlos proudly admitted. "I got a little side business where I, you know, fill orders."

"I'm looking for a gun," Nice articulated, interested in the look on his face.

"I can help you with that," Carlos assured him. "What caliber?"

"I'm looking for a machine gun."

Carlos ruminated for a moment on Nice's request. He pulled on his bottom lip several times.

"That kinda hardware is high-end, expensive, and you wouldn't want to be caught with it in your possession," Carlos shared.

"I'm not worried about any of that stuff. Can you help me?"

"I can't," Carlos voiced, "but I know a guy. It would be expensive. At least a grand, maybe fifteen hundred."

"So, is that one thousand dollars to one thousand, five hundred dollars?"

"Yeah."

"I can do that," Nice admitted.

"All right. Let me make a phone call."

Carlos retrieved his cell phone from the pocket of his coveralls and called a number from his phone log. Nice listened to Carlos as he spoke Spanish into the phone.

"Tomorrow, 3:30 in San Marcos," Carlos told Nice as he momentarily took the phone away from his head. "I'll give you the details in a minute." Carlos returned to his Spanish-speaking call.

Nice believed that his plan was about to take a monumental leap. Now, all he would need was access to a time machine.

CHAPTER 19

Wayne Patterson was the lone occupant of the chapel located within the Palomar Medical Center. The room was not very big, perhaps twenty feet by twenty feet with five rows containing six chairs each and six kneelers at the front of the chapel. A crucifix hung in the center of the front of the room.

The room was clean and sterile. Its attempt to accommodate all religions made it appear as if it did not accommodate any religion. Within a minute, it could be transformed into a game room.

Wayne stared at the floor and occasionally looked out the window at the late afternoon sky. Every once in a while, he would look at the door, wondering when they were going to come to tell him his daughter was dead.

It was while he was peering out the window that his concentration was broken.

"Can I sit with you?" his wife, Marion, asked from the doorway.

Wayne nodded with a forced smile.

"How is she?" he inquired, knowing exactly how she was twenty minutes earlier when he was with her.

"She finally fell asleep," Marion answered. Wayne had no response.

Wayne took a handkerchief from his pants pocket and wiped a touch of moisture from his eye.

"Would you like to say some prayers together?" Marion's voice was kind and compassionate.

"No," Wayne said conclusively. "I don't want to pray anymore. It's useless."

"Don't say that," she interjected, objecting to his comment.

"No. More and more I wonder if there is a God. Maybe we are just evolved animals that are mental slaves to the fear of an all-powerful being. We feel guilty because of how much we would enjoy a hedonistic lifestyle."

"Wayne, you don't believe that."

"I don't think I believe anything anymore," Wayne remarked, looking forward without focus. "You know, when I was a kid, I was the best altar boy at Immaculate Conception Church in Charles City, Iowa. They called me for weddings. They called me for funerals. They called me when the Bishop would come to visit. You know why?"

Marion shook her head in a negative manner.

"Because I memorized the entire mass, word for word. And when I spoke the words, I was like a great orator, filled with the Holy Spirit. I said those words with passion and conviction because I believed Jesus was there with me and I was taking part in the celebration of his life and resurrection."

"But now, I'm given one baby and I have to watch her rot to death. Maybe that altar boy was a fool, or a great actor, or just a player in a grand charade. From where I stand, it's hard for me to believe there is a God."

Wayne finally turned to look at Marion.

"I apologize for my rambling. I've got no one else to talk to. You don't know how much I want to believe."

"When you were praying you had someone to talk to. Faith will get us through this," Marion conveyed to him. "I know it will."

Marion walked over to him and Wayne stood. They embraced and Wayne began to sob. And so did Marion.

CHAPTER 20

Darkness enveloped Carlsbad. Deborah Wilkinson was a cashier at the Walmart on Marron Road in Oceanside, just north of the Oceanside/Carlsbad border. She had worked there for nearly three years and found it to be an easy, yet monotonous, job.

Deborah was twenty-seven years old, 5 feet 5 inches tall, 121 pounds with a short, brunette, wedge hairdo. Her hairstyle was selected based on its ease of maintenance. She did not believe in makeup. Deborah was never trying to impress anyone. She tried to make every decision and function in her life have some degree of utility.

The store closed at 10:00 pm, but her shift at Walmart ended at 11:00 pm this day and by 11:07 pm, she was in the parking lot unlocking her car door. Deborah drove a red, late model Mazda 2.

Deborah lived in an apartment complex located on the corner of Seascape Drive and Camino de las Ondas, a street that was quite close to the duplex Nice shared with his mother. Deborah had a roommate, who was a kindergarten teacher at a nearby public grade school.

On this day, Deborah wore a Merona long-sleeve, v-neck t-shirt, black, tapered, zip front pants, and a gray crewneck sweatshirt.

On her feet, she wore black and white, patterned, Loretta loafer sneakers.

Deborah lived approximately six and a half miles from the Walmart and the traffic was always extremely light at this time of night. She drove down College Boulevard, which turned into Cannon Road. All the while, her mind was on autopilot, wondering what she was going to have for dinner and if she had clean clothes for tomorrow.

At the corner of Cannon Road and Faraday Avenue was a traffic light. There was hardly any housing or commercial development around this area. It was one of the few, large, open and undeveloped areas of Carlsbad. There was an apartment complex on one corner, but the buildings were set back from the road.

As Deborah waited for the light to turn green, she heard the screeching of tires. As she checked her rear-view mirror, she felt the impact. It wasn't really that hard and none of the airbags deployed. She put the car in park and debated for a moment whether or not to get out of the car. The other driver was standing in the road, clearly distressed, and came to her window.

"Are you all right?" a young, clean-shaven man asked. "I'm so sorry. I wasn't paying attention."

Deborah opened her car door and stepped out. She examined the damage and saw that her rear bumper was slightly pressed in.

"We should exchange insurance information," the man told her.

As they spoke, a white Dodge van pulled up along the side of them, essentially blocking the view of Deborah and the man from any passing traffic. The driver of the van had rolled down the passenger window. Deborah looked at the driver through the window. The driver began to speak.

"I saw the whole thing. I'll give you my name as a . . ."

Before he could say the word, 'witness,' Deborah was grabbed from behind. Molech had suddenly appeared like a wraith in the night. With a quick hook move, Molech's hand covered her mouth and the jet injector vaccine gun filled with vecuronium bromide was pressed against her neck and the trigger pulled. With military precision, the sliding side door of the van opened and she was handed to three men inside. Her effort to struggle quickly ceased.

One of the men in the back of the van stepped out and got into Deborah's car. He handed Molech her purse and Molech walked back to the car that struck Deborah's and got in. All three vehicles took off in a westbound direction.

Shortly, Deborah Wilkinson would meet Sheila DeLucia, the first abductee.

CHAPTER 21

The daily mass at St. Elizabeth Seton took place, most of the time, not in the large church, but rather in a chapel located behind the altar of the main church. The chapel provided an intimate setting and allowed for more socializing after mass.

A sign on the wall of the chapel claimed it could hold 177 people, but there was only seating for 78 people. There was also an organ in the back of the chapel. The front wall contained a crucifix and stained-glass window. The window was surrounded by small statues of each of the twelve apostles, including Matthias, the apostle who replaced Judas Iscariot.

Every day, the mass at Saint Elizabeth Seton church drew a standing room only crowd and for those who attended 'regularly,' they always sat in the same chairs. Nice, Sally, and Yappy sat in the front row. Ben and Theresa, who were accompanied this day for the first time by Chelbi, sat in the second to the last row. Betty and Bob Rondolay sat in the second row from the front and Wayne and Marion sat four rows from the back row.

Chelbi's transformation under the tutelage of Betty Rondolay was striking. No longer did she appear like a teenager who hangs out at a mall. She now appeared to be more comparable to a waif-like model, turning heads when she entered the room. Chelbi wore a plum Jessica Howard, petite, necklace-detailed draped dress, with a matching handbag and black American Rag Meesha, Mary Jane wedge shoes.

Of all the clothes that Betty purchased for Chelbi, this outfit had the best fit. The rest of the clothes were brought to a seamstress for modification to fit Chelbi's petite frame.

In addition, her makeup gave her facial features a highlight and glow. Her hair was now slightly shorter, but perfectly coifed for her face.

Chelbi had not been to church since high school and she was making an effort to become re-indoctrinated to her religion.

Every mass included a five to seven minute homily, presented by the pastor, Father Tom Hayes that generally provided a moralizing discourse on the day's Gospel and Scripture readings.

As the mass this Wednesday was coming to a close, Father Hayes had a comment before the final blessing.

"As you're fleeing church today, feel free to take a pot of flowers from the narthex."

These were flowers that decorated the altar during Easter masses and they would be located in the vestibule area between the outside door and the entrance to the church.

For some reason, Father Tom's comment about 'fleeing church' pushed a button in Wayne Patterson. During the final song, Father Tom would leave after the first chorus and the congregants would sing one additional chorus.

As soon as the second chorus of the song concluded, Wayne took off and made a beeline directly to the sacristy, the area of the church where the priest dresses for mass.

Wayne entered the room as Father Tom was slipping off his vestments. He began to speak before Father Tom knew who was in the room.

"Father," Wayne said in a strident tone, "you may think it's funny to say that the people attending daily mass are fleeing church, but no one in that room ever flees. We want to be here and we're in no hurry to leave."

"Wayne, I only say it to get people's attention," Father Tom said in his defense. "I'm sorry if it offends you."

"Well it does," Wayne's voice was seething with anger. "Why don't you save it for the hypocrites who only come on Easter and Christmas? Instead of kissing their rear ends. You should appreciate the people who make this place what it is. And you should talk! You race outta there like the place is on fire. What are you afraid that somebody is going to talk to you? Ask you to say a prayer for them? You know, for a priest, you're pretty cold."

Father Tom just looked at Wayne.

"I'm a sinner, Wayne. I'm imperfect. I strive for perfection." The men stared at each other for a moment. "Did Marion tell you that I saw Joy yesterday?" the priest asked.

"She did," Wayne advised with his voice pulling back from its tirade. He then added, "Thank you."

Wayne turned and retreated from the room, almost without direction, wondering what he was saying and what he was doing there.

After Wayne exited the sacristy, Marion entered and saw Father Tom.

"I don't know what he said Father, but I'm sorry. He's been under a lot of stress lately."

"I understand. I'll pray for him. And Joy. And you," the priest replied with a smile.

"Thank you, Father," Marion sincerely conveyed.

Marion knew the probable outcome for her daughter, Joy. But she had a greater concern for the outcome of her husband.

CHAPTER 22

It was 9:45 am at Ben's Glassworks. Ben, Nice, Diz, and Lozo met to discuss the agenda for the day's activities. Ben put on his reading glasses and grabbed a clipboard, which contained a list of the jobs for the day, prepared by Ben's wife, Theresa.

These meetings generally took place in the middle of the shop, without any structure. Ben perused the list, then appeared to have remembered something. He took off his glasses and looked at Diz.

"Diz?" Ben exclaimed.

"What?" Diz asked in a nonchalant manner and readjusted his Chicago Cubs baseball cap.

"You were supposed to bring the donuts," Ben reminded him.

"Benny, there were too many people. Why can't you or Nice do it?"

"I told you," Ben conveyed as if Diz should be well aware of the information. "My wife won't let me stop there on the way back from church. If Nice goes, his mother will rat me out to my wife."

"Benny, I'll bring donuts tomorrow," Lozo told him.

"All right," Ben said with a frustrated smile.

Ben returned his focus to the jobs list.

"Lozo, the Geisserelli job is back on," Ben conveyed.

"I know. Our guys are there and mobilized. I am gonna get over there and see if we can pick up the pace," Lozo told them as he walked toward the door. "Hey Nice," he spoke up to grab Nice's attention, "I gotta bounce."

"Later, *esé*," Nice acknowledged his comment and Lozo gave him a thumbs up.

Ben immediately returned to the jobs list.

"We got the sealant in for the curtain wall repair at that building on Palomar Oaks Way," Ben informed Diz. "They called yesterday and said the glass was there. Can you and Nice go take care of it today?"

A curtain wall system is an exterior covering of a building that is non-structural, generally made of lightweight materials, such as aluminum, to house glass panes that are resistant to the environment. It gives the appearance of a wall of glass.

"Might as well," Diz uttered.

Nice knew from the lack of enthusiasm in Diz's response that he really did not want to go.

"You want me and Lozo to go do it this afternoon?" Nice offered to Ben.

"On a curtain wall system, you gotta be certified," Ben explained. "Diz is the only one of us to be certified."

"Education is vastly overrated," Diz announced. "Why don't we get Nice certified?"

"Let me know next time they offer a class and we'll do it," Ben declared. Nice smiled, grateful for the faith Ben had in him.

"Okay Nice, we're going to take a ride on a swing stage today. You know what that is?" Diz asked.

"Isn't that the device that window washers use that hangs from the top of a building, like a platform?"

"That's it. Get two safety harnesses," Diz relayed beginning his order, "two vertical ropes with the lanyards and gloves. You feeling strong today, boy?"

"Yeah," Nice answered with a smile.

"Good. Because I'm not. So get a handtruck and grab the come-along." Diz had one more comment. "Throw the stuff in your truck, because I don't feel like driving."

Nice moved quickly to fill Diz's order. The work day had begun.

CHAPTER 23

It was nearing 11:00 am and Detective Wayne Patterson was sitting in his cubicle at Carlsbad Police Headquarters running the name 'Molech' and its various permutations through identification databases without any luck. He was considering contacting the FBI when his partner, Andy Sandoval, appeared at his cubicle.

Wayne looked at Andy and he knew the information was not going to be good.

"Dispatch got a call this morning about a missing girl," Andy shared. "Her roommate said she never made it home last night."

Wayne's mind began to race as he leaned back in his chair.

"When was the last time somebody saw her?" Wayne asked with genuine concern.

"She was working at the Walmart off College Boulevard last night. She got off her shift at eleven o'clock."

"Let's not wait the twenty-four hours. Get an APB out on her and her car. Then let's go to Walmart to look at the surveillance video on the parking lot."

Normally, the police would not commence a missing person's investigation until twenty-four hours after a person was reported missing. In this case, Wayne ordered an 'all-points bulletin' immediately, so that all law enforcement personnel within the county could commence looking for Deborah Wilkinson.

"One other thing:" Andy wanted to add, "A patrol officer just called in. Your buddy, Zeke, wants to talk to you. He's near where we saw him the other day."

Zeke was the homeless man who informed Wayne about the plot to abduct the three girls and provided him with the name, Molech, as the local man plotting the abductions.

"All right," Wayne said as he rose from his chair while lifting his sport coat that rested on the back of it. "You go to Walmart and I'll go talk to Zeke. I think I want to talk to the roommate."

"She's in the conference room right now."

"Let's go talk to her."

Wayne moved without deviation directly to the conference room near the entrance to the headquarters. There waiting for him was Shelley Palmer, a twenty-eight year old kindergarten teacher at the Pacific Rim Elementary School. Shelly was 5 feet 6 inches tall, 140 pounds, with long brunette hair that she wore in a ponytail. She wore a Style & Co. gray, marled, ribbed-knit, sweater dress with black stockings and black, Easy Spirit Norden Flats shoes.

Wayne and Andy entered the room and Andy was the first to speak.

"Miss Palmer, this is Detective Patterson."

"It's nice to meet you, Miss Palmer. We want to do what we can to find Deborah immediately."

"I thought she came in last night," Shelley conveyed. "I go to bed early, because I have to be up early."

"Did she have a boyfriend or a man in her life?" Wayne wondered.

"No," Shelley shook her head. "She had absolutely no interest in men."

"What about women?" Andy inquired.

"No," Shelley added conclusively. "Anything lesbian or gay would be a sin. And she would have nothing to do with that."

"Was she religious?" Wayne queried.

"That was the number one thing in her life. She didn't do anything social. When she had time, she would read her Bible. If she wasn't working or home, she would be at St. Patrick's Church, off Tamarack. She got involved with a lot of different clubs there."

Wayne paused for a moment to think about anything else he would like to ask her. Right now though, he wanted to get to Zeke.

"If you can think of anything else that might help us find her," Wayne advised handing her his business card, "call me."

Shelley placed his card in her purse and the three of them headed to their appointed destinations.

CHAPTER 24

As Nice and Diz left the parking lot outside Ben's Glassworks, Diz picked up Nice's Bible and began looking at the dog-eared pages that were highlighted and written upon.

"Looks like you enjoy the good book," Diz observed.

"I do. I call it my roadmap. It helps me get where I want to go," Nice advised.

"My favorite time of the week is when I'm in church," Diz shared.

"Where's your church?" Nice wondered.

"The Greater Victory Baptist Church on South 29th Street in San Diego. My wife plays the organ. Would you like to come with me sometime?" Diz offered.

"I'd like that. And you're always welcome at my church."

"I've been to your church many times. Benny wouldn't have it any other way. When you get to heaven, do you think you'll see me there?" Diz speculated.

"You know what I think," Nice spoke with a wide smile, "when you get to heaven, save me a seat."

Diz appreciated the comment.

"I think the same thing as you," Diz speculated. "It's not so much the religion as the life you lead. A good person is a good person. So, here's the deal. When you get to heaven, if I'm not there, you go lookin' for me."

"It's a deal," Nice agreed, sealing the pledge with another smile.

Diz glanced out the window and Nice changed the topic.

"Why do we need the safety harnesses if they have a swing stage?"

"It's because of OSHA. You know what that is?" Diz paused for a moment. "The federal government safety guidelines. Anything over ten feet off the ground, you gotta have a safety harness."

"What do you connect the ropes to?" Nice wondered.

"They have anchor mounts on the roof. That's what we will connect the ropes or vertical lifelines to."

"Diz, you're a smart guy. Lozo was telling me you got like a real high degree in school."

"I always enjoyed learning. My dad would say all the time, try to learn something new every day. Because the day you stop learning, should be the day they put you in the ground."

"Can I ask you a question about something?" Nice requested.

"Sure." Diz was quick to respond.

"Do you know anything about time travel?"

"I know there's a lot of theories out there," Diz responded. "As to whether or not it's possible, I can't say."

"Do you know where I could find out?" Nice inquired.

"Yeah," Diz answered quickly. "I know a guy who is a physics professor down at UCSD. I'll call him later and see if you can go in and talk to him."

Diz was referring to the University of California at San Diego, one of the schools in the California public university system.

"Thanks a lot, Diz. That would be great." Then Nice added, "You're such a smart guy, why are you working for a glass business?"

"I learned a long time ago, Nicean, my friend, that life is short. So, you better do what you enjoy. You know Benny is the best. I'd rather cut glass with him and enjoy it, than do something else and be miserable."

Nice always enjoyed Diz's common sense approach to life. He felt blessed and grateful that he worked with men who were so understanding and so willing to share and teach.

CHAPTER 25

As Wayne drove northbound on Roosevelt Avenue in downtown Carlsbad, just beyond Grand Avenue, he spotted Zeke pushing his grocery cart. Zeke's hair looked a little cleaner and his clothes were less ragged than two days earlier. Wayne pulled up to the curb beside him and rolled down the passenger window.

"Hey, Zeke," Wayne called out to get his attention.

Zeke looked toward his voice and a big smile filled his face.

"Detective Wayne," Zeke called out, maneuvering his cart to bring it closer to Wayne's car.

"You look like you took a shower since the last time I saw you."

"I made it down to the beach. They got those public showers. Just as good as the indoor ones," Zeke conveyed.

"What's going on, my friend?" Wayne inquired.

Like he did the last time, Zeke looked up and down the street, then leaned against the passenger door of the car, sticking his head slightly into the car. His bad breath wafted into the vehicle.

"I heard they grabbed the second girl. The third one is gonna be grabbed by Friday," Zeke was slow and serious.

"Do you have a name by chance?" Wayne wondered.

"Not for the girl," Zeke shared. "But I got the name of the guy who ordered the three girls to be jacked. His name is Feardesin. F-E-A-R-D-E-S-I-N. I don't know his first name, but he's from outta town."

"Where are these guys hanging out?"

"I don't know," Zeke answered and shrugged his shoulders.

"Where are you getting your information?" Wayne pressed.

"I sleep behind a lot of bars," Zeke confessed. "I always feel safe there. The stuff I'm giving you came from conversations that I overheard in the parking lots. But I can't remember the names of the bars. I didn't want anybody to see me, so I either tried to stay out of sight or under my box. I don't know what they look like."

"All right," Wayne said as he reached for his wallet. He once again removed a twenty dollar bill. "You hear anything else, you know how to get a hold of me." Wayne folded the money and gave him a final admonition before relinquishing it to him. "No liquor, no dope. Okay?"

"Boy Scout's honor," Zeke replied with a smile. "Thank you kindly for your generosity. It is much appreciated."

Wayne pulled away from the curb and shared a final wave with Zeke. He was left with only one question: Who is Feardesin?

CHAPTER 26

Around 2:30 pm, Nice and Diz were pulling into the parking lot of Ben's Glassworks after successfully installing a new exterior glass panel on a curtain wall system of a commercial office building.

"Nice, you did good today," Diz said. "That glass panel was heavy."

"I wanna thank you, Diz. I learned a lot."

"When we get inside, I'll call that professor I know down at UCSD. I'll see if he can make time for you."

"Thanks a lot, Diz. I'd really appreciate it."

Nice realized that he was supposed to be in San Marcos at 3:30 to speak with someone named Treese about a machine gun. Nice parked the truck and Diz started to remove some tools from the bed of the truck.

"Don't worry about it, Diz. I'll put all the stuff back," Nice told him.

"Whatever you say," Diz replied and both men entered the shop.

Ben was in his office going over paperwork and Nice walked in with a quick question.

"I've got to run an errand over in San Marcos. Do you need anything?"

"Nah," Ben conveyed. "It's been pretty quiet. Will you be back before five o'clock? Otherwise, I'll shut everything down."

"No, I'll be back," Nice assured him.

"Okay," Ben acknowledged. "I'll see you later."

Nice wanted to say goodbye to Diz, but he was in the men's room. Nice left the shop headed for San Marcos. On his way, he would stop at a branch of Wells Fargo Bank to withdraw two thousand dollars to cover the potential cost of the gun.

CHAPTER 27

Within thirty minutes, Nice arrived at Sacco Tool & Dye located on Bent Avenue, just off San Marcos Boulevard. This section of town was a hodge-podge of various commercial buildings including retail stores, auto repair shops, and local fast food restaurants.

Sacco Tool & Dye set back approximately 100 feet from the street. It could not be seen from the street and was nestled behind a furniture warehouse. Nice drove down the driveway and parked in one of the four parking spaces reserved for customers.

Nice walked in and the dirt and dust were thick within the small reception area. The air was permeated by oil products. The reception area was ten feet by ten feet and had a raised countertop parallel to the back wall that cut the room in half. Behind the counter sat an obese woman, approximately 280 pounds with a yellow Muumuu-type of dress draped over her.

"Excuse me," Nice interjected to get her attention. "Is Treese here? I have an appointment."

"Hold on," she said with a thick, Spanish accent. Then she picked up the phone and dialed two numbers. She spoke quickly to the party on the other end.

When she was done with her quick conversation, she returned the receiver to its cradle and told Nice, "You can go back. I'll buzz you in."

The woman then pushed a button and a buzz could be heard coming from a solid, tan, metal door to the left of Nice. He entered the work area.

This area was a cacophony of loud sounds, sparks from welders, and Spanish music.

"Hey," a man yelled out to Nice across the room. "Over here."

The man who called Nice was 5 feet 10 inches tall, 190 pounds, with black, close-cropped hair and a small line of hair that ran from under his bottom lip to the area under his chin. He wore a green, weathered t-shirt, with various grease marks and black, denim jeans. On his feet, he wore black, steel-toe, CAT boots.

Nice approached the man with a smile. He believed that his goal of going back in time to the day of Jesus' crucifixion, was about to take a giant step forward.

"I'm Treese. How you doing? You're Carlos' friend? From Carlsbad?"

"Yeah. I'm Nice. Peace be with you."

"You know Carlos told me your name was Nice, but I didn't think I heard him right."

"I get that a lot," Nice shared.

"I understand you're interested in some heavy duty hardware. Correct?"

"Yeah."

"Well, you know, that kind of hardware is not cheap. Thirteen hundred dollars. Can you do that or is it gonna be a problem?"

"No problem," Nice assured him. "I can do it."

"I need to ask you a couple of questions. You wearing a wire?"

Nice had watched enough television shows to know what Treese was talking about.

"No," Nice told him succinctly.

"Okay. Raise your shirt." Nice complied and lifted his blue Ben's Glassworks t-shirt to the top of his chest. "Turn around." Nice again complied with a 360 degree turn. "Put your shirt down."

Treese paused for a moment. "You slamming glass?" he asked.

Nice was stumped. Treese was asking him if he was using methamphetamines. Nice did not have a quick answer.

"You know I work for a glass place and I heard that term one time on an episode of *Cops*. I didn't know what it meant then, and I don't know what it means now."

"Don't worry about it," Treese informed him. "Listen, if we do business, you're not gonna go shoot up a school or a mall, are you?"

"No," Nice assured him. "I don't want anyone to get hurt."

"So, you just want one of these things. Is that it?"

"Yeah."

"One final thing: The only way I'll sell to you is if you give me your word that you won't tell anyone, especially the police, where you got it." Treese was serious. "You give me your word?"

"I give you my word," Nice declared.

Treese looked at Nice and thought he was odd, but his money was green. He walked over to a metal cabinet, approximately five feet high, covered with stickers from Champion spark plugs that hung on a concrete wall, approximately eighteen inches off the ground. Treese opened the cabinet and reached up on the side of one of the higher shelves and appeared to pull on a lever.

The cabinet then pivoted on one side, where an unseen hinge was connected. Behind the cabinet, the blocks covered by the cabinet were removed and there was now access to another room on the other side of the wall.

Both men stepped over the bottom three rows of blocks into the darkened room and Treese turned on the lights. The room was approximately twenty feet wide and eighty feet long. At the end where the men were standing, there was a workbench with four drawers that ran the entire length of the bench. On each of the three walls at their end hung a gun rack. One rack included tactical shotguns, another included tactical rifles, and the third contained smaller-sized machine guns.

As Nice looked around, Treese pulled the metal cabinet back in place to cover the opening where they entered. The walls were covered in soundproofing material. Approximately sixty feet of the room comprised a shooting range, complete with a slope of dirt at the far end and retractable target system to allow a shooter to send a target downrange and then pull it back to examine their proficiency with a particular firearm.

"Before we go any farther," Treese announced, "can I see the cash?"

Nice reached into his pocket and pulled out a wad of twenty $100 bills. He counted off thirteen of them and placed the money on the workbench.

"Let me show you what I got. You want a suppressor on it? A silencer?"

"No. I want it loud," Nice conveyed.

Diz retrieved a gun from the machine gun rack and brought it over to Nice.

"This is a MAC-10. Holds thirty bullets in the clip. That's about a two-second pull on the trigger. It comes with a suppressor, but you can screw it off. When you're not using it, keep the safety on."

Treese handed the gun to Nice, who looked at it as if he was not sure what to do with it.

"I'll take this one," Nice said quickly.

"Good," Treese acknowledged and he opened one of the drawers on the workbench looking for something. The first drawer he opened was filled with revolver handguns. The second drawer was filled with semi-automatic handguns. The third drawer was filled with various ammunition and targets, which is what Treese sought. The fourth drawer was filled with various clips or magazines for all of the guns.

Treese took out a light brown target, which was the outline of a man. He connected it to the wired target system and sent it downrange.

"What are you doing?" Nice inquired.

"You're going to test it. All sales are final. No refunds."

Treese gave Nice a pair a shooting 'ears,' which were earmuffs, to minimize the sound of the gun and a pair of shooting glasses. Treese also donned these items.

"With a machine gun," Treese started his shooting lesson, "only the first shot really has any accuracy. After that, you just hope you're hitting your target. Okay. Check the safety."

Nice moved the safety from the off position and outstretched his right hand, pointing the gun downrange.

"Hold it," Treese stopped him. "You're a big guy. And you could probably handle it one-handed. But in here use two hands. I don't want you to hit a light or the target wires."

Nice brought his right elbow in tight next to his chest and put his left hand in front of his right hand near the trigger.

"How's it feel?" Treese asked.

"Good," Nice answered, not really knowing how it should feel.

"This thing on top is the bolt. Pull it back and it's ready to dance."

Nice pulled the bolt back with his left hand and repositioned the gun. He looked at the target and pulled the trigger.

The gun viciously rained bullets and the deafening sound of gunfire was over within three seconds. All that was left was the resonating echo of bullets exploding from their shells and the gun smoke that filled the air.

Both men stared downrange and Treese lifted his protective glasses to his forehead. Nice had put a horizontal line through the center of the target and cut it in half.

"You're a natural," Treese told him. "I'm gonna give you two loaded clips and something to carry it in."

Treese was impressed and Nice was ready to change history.

Part 2

CHAPTER 28

On this Wednesday evening, Nice found himself again sitting on his back porch and browsing through his Bible. The setting sun was in front of him and layers of magnificent hues filled the sky. Yappy sat comfortably in his lap, just enjoying being with Nice.

Nice's mother, Sally, called out from the kitchen.

"Nice, where's your sister?"

"She's here, with me," he replied.

"Okay. I'm going to go," Sally spoke through the sliding screen door. "I should be back by nine o'clock."

On Wednesday nights, Sally attended a Bible study class at the church.

"See'ya ma," Nice replied.

Shortly after Sally left, the phone rang. Nice and Yappy went inside and Nice answered the phone on the kitchen wall.

"Hello," he announced.

"Hi, is this Nice?" a female voice asked.

"Yes, it is," he pleasantly advised.

"This is Chelbi. How are you doing?"

"I'm doing well. Peace be with you. How are you?"

"I'm fine. Listen, I was wondering if you would like to go for an ice cream somewhere? My grandfather said he would treat us."

"I think it's a good idea. But he doesn't have to treat us. Ask him if he would like to go."

"I already did and he said 'No.' I think my grandmother helped influence his answer."

"I would have to bring my sister with us," Nice informed Chelbi.

"Your sister?" Chelbi replied, wondering what he was talking about. "Oh, your dog. She's great. I look forward to it."

"All right. We'll be at your place in a few minutes."

"Would you like me to drive?" Chelbi asked.

"No. I can drive."

"Thank you. I don't really enjoy driving in Southern California."

"It's no problem," Nice assured her. "I'm on my way."

CHAPTER 29

Nice, Chelbi, and Yappy sat in a booth at the Dairy Queen on Encinitas Boulevard in Encinitas, California, the city immediately to the south of Carlsbad. Chelbi ordered a small, Oreo Blizzard and Nice had a small, soft-serve, vanilla cone that he would occasionally allow Yappy to lick. No one in the restaurant seemed to mind that Nice had Yappy sitting on his arm.

"What does your mom do for a living?" Chelbi inquired.

"She's a receptionist at a chiropractor's office," Nice shared. "They allow her to bring my sister to work."

After a few moments of silence, Nice decided it was his turn to ask a question. "Do they have Dairy Queens where you live?" Nice inquired.

"Yeah, but I don't think you can sit inside like this," Chelbi replied.

"Your grandfather and I come down here every once in a while," Nice told her. "He gets the exact same ice cream that you got, but he gets the larger size."

"He really likes you," Chelbi disclosed to Nice.

"I really like him. I love him. He's the kind of man I hope to be," Nice sincerely commented.

"I want to apologize for the other night in the bar." Now, it was Chelbi's turn to be sincere.

"Forget about it," Nice told her with a smile.

"Do you know why I'm here in Carlsbad?" Chelbi posed her inquiry.

"I would like to think it's because you love your grandparents," Nice believed.

"Back home in Kansas, I was working minimum wage jobs. I had no interest in going to school and I blamed everyone else for my situation, but myself. I started to rebel. I would go drinking and based on my size, it didn't take long to get liquored up. One night, somebody slips something in my drink. The next thing I know these guys are holding me down in the men's room, pulling my underwear off and tearing at my shirt. A guy comes in from nowhere and starts busting heads, so I wasn't raped. But after that, I couldn't live in Kansas anymore. Every man looked like the guy who was on top of me." She paused for a moment and looked down at the table. "So, that's why I'm in Carlsbad."

"Did you ever meet the guy who saved you?" Nice asked.

"I didn't. I wish I did."

"They say miracles happen every day," Nice professed. "All around us. You just have to be looking."

"Maybe you can help me with that," Chelbi asked, looking like a lonely little girl.

"Deal." Nice extended his hand to her and they shook.

"You never told me what you were looking up in those encyclopedias that day."

Chelbi was referring to Nice's search on Easter through Ben's outdated encyclopedias for information on time travel.

"I'd rather not talk about it," Nice expressed.

"Com'on. I just told you something personal about me. Com'on. Please. Pretty please," Chelbi begged.

"If I tell you, you promise you're not going to laugh?"

"I promise," she declared.

"I want to go back in time to the day that Jesus was crucified and I want to help him. I don't want to stop it, I just can't stand the thought of such a good person being brutalized."

Chelbi looked at Nice without expression.

"And how do you plan on doing this?"

"I was researching time travel. I believe that if I can just go back in time, I can hold off the Roman Army or at least get them to stop beating him."

"The Roman Army is just going to listen to you?"

"No. I'm going to bring a machine gun with me."

Chelbi was speechless. She did have an observational comment.

"You know what? I think that is crazy. But I like crazy. Nicean, count me in."

Her comment brought a big smile to Nice's face.

"Listen, you can't tell anybody. Okay? Promise me."

"I promise," Chelbi declared. "Now, where are we going to find a time machine?"

"I've got an appointment on Thursday to talk to this physics professor down at UCSD. He's a friend of Diz, from work. If anybody knows, he will."

"What about the machine gun?" Chelbi said in a tone obviously questioning his ability to obtain one.

Nice looked around and leaned in toward her. She mimicked his action. He then said in a low voice, "I've already got it."

Chelbi looked at him with her mouth open.

"You got a machine gun?" she quizzed, in a quiet voice and with a shake of her head.

Nice nodded affirmatively.

"I have greatly underestimated you, my friend," Chelbi proudly informed him. "That is truly gangster."

Nice was excited that he now had someone to conspire with him to alter history. Chelbi had a new appreciation of Nice. Perhaps, he was not as innocent as he seemed.

CHAPTER 30

At the Semany Floral Warehouse, Molech and his men were discussing a strategy for their next and final abduction. This one would take place during the day, so added precautions were going to be taken in the event of any unwanted intervention. The discussions were disrupted by the ring of Molech's cellular phone.

Molech looked at the Caller ID and immediately spoke up in a raised voice, "Everybody shut up!" He then answered the phone.

"Yes."

"Mr. Molech. It's Mr. Feardesin. I'm pleased with your progress. Are the packages still in pristine condition?" His voice was slow and meted.

"They're fine," Molech answered.

"They better be," Feardesin commanded. "Now, because our little endeavor is almost complete, I want you to understand that *anything* that may attempt to interrupt your progress, must be dealt with most harshly. Burn it all down. There is no going back now. No relenting. But make sure those packages are untouched. Do you understand my instructions?"

"I understand them," Molech conceded.

"I'm sure that you do. I am holding you to a very high standard, Mr. Molech. Don't disappoint me."

"I won't."

"Make sure your men know what to do in the event of any impediments."

"They'll know how to handle it."

"Very good. I hope that we can meet one day," Feardesin said.

"I would like that," Molech uttered.

"The transport trailer will be there on Friday afternoon. A truck will come and pick it up closer to ten o'clock at night."

"Very good," Molech informed him.

"Goodbye, Mr. Molech." With that, the call ended.

Molech, turned his attention to the six other men standing in the room, attempting to look like they were not interested in Molech's phone call.

"We got to make sure everybody's strapped," Molech barked.

Molech wanted to make sure everyone was carrying some type of weapon.

"Let's go over it again," Molech announced, referring to the plan for the final abduction.

In his dealings with Feardesin, Molech believed that he could never be overly prepared.

CHAPTER 31

Nice, Chelbi and Yappy were headed home on the northbound Interstate 5 freeway and departed the freeway at the Poinsettia Drive off-ramp. At the top of the ramp was a stop light and Nice stopped with two cars ahead of him.

On the corner of the ramp and Poinsettia Drive was a homeless man. Nice was taking an unusual amount of time looking at him and suddenly realized who he was. It was the same homeless man that he gave a soda and his mother's prepared lunch to near the Jack-in-the-Box restaurant. He wore the same pea coat and military, green pants. His hair and beard looked a little dirtier and his complexion was sunburned. He still carried the same weathered, handwritten sign that said, in block letters, 'ANYTHING WILL HELP.'

"Just ignore them and they don't bother you," Chelbi instructed him.

Nice took out his wallet, pulled out a five dollar bill, and rolled down his window.

"Hey," Nice called out and waved the man over. The man moved quickly to Nice's truck, concerned about the stoplight turning green.

Nice handed him the five dollar bill and told him, "Peace be with you."

"Thank you," the man said sincerely and Nice's eyes were drawn to his green eyes.

"Nice, the light is green," Chelbi told him. Nice refocused and started to drive off, giving the homeless man a quick wave.

"Do you think that guy would help you?" Chelbi asked with a slightly annoyed tone.

"I would like to think he would if I was homeless. I'm grateful for my blessings and I want to share with others whenever I can. A great man I know likes to say, "You gotta do what's right. Because what's right is right.""

"That sounds like my grandfather, Ben Krische, talking," Chelbi noted.

"And this sounds like Nicean Bevilacqua listening."

Within twenty minutes, Chelbi was dropped off and Nice and Yappy were entering through the door of their home. The lights were on, so Nice automatically assumed that his mother had also returned home. Nice set Yappy down and she took off in search of her mommy.

Nice walked into the kitchen and Sally was sitting at the kitchen table. Sally wore a blue and ivory square-links pattern blouse and Talbots weekend embroidered anchor chino pants.

"Hi, ma," Nice casually told her with a smile. Nice could tell by the look on his mother's face that she was agitated about something. "What's wrong?"

"Where were you?" Sally demanded.

"I went for an ice cream." Nice answered, wondering 'what was the big deal?'

"Who did you go with?"

"Chelbi and Yappy."

"I don't want you going anywhere with that girl. Do you understand me?"

"Why?" Nice's response was indignant.

"Girls like that are trouble and you don't need trouble. I have spent my entire life keeping you away from trouble and I will not have it thrown away by some little tramp." Sally's statement was definitive.

"Ma, how can you say that?" Nice was incredulous. "That is not Christian. Don't you listen to Father Tom? Judge not lest ye be judged? You're the one who taught me what the Bible says. And it doesn't say to pass judgment on people."

"She called you, right? That's how it starts. A man is supposed to call a woman, not the other way around. These girls today have loose morals. You don't know the whole story about her."

"Yes, I do. She told me. I know all about what happened to her in Kansas. She's a nice person."

"Oh, so now she's trying to play the sympathy card. And she's got you under her spell. Nicean," Sally's voice was raising with frustrated exasperation, "you don't know the ways of the world."

"And why is that?" Nicean flared, with raised voice, reaching a boiling point. "You did such a good job of keeping the world away from me that I can't function in it. If it wasn't for Ben, you would probably keep me locked in a closet all day, because *everything* is part of the world, run by the devil, so let's keep Nice away from it. When I do have to deal with it, I feel like I am on a different planet."

"Don't raise your voice. It upsets your sister," Sally retorted, referring to Yappy.

"Ma, something tells me you don't like to hear the truth. You like to tell everybody that I'm special. Different. 'Oh, he doesn't understand.' You want to talk about Chelbi playing the sympathy card? You're a professional at it. You love that everybody feels bad for you because you have to take care of that big, dumb, dimwit son of yours, who probably is going to have to be institutionalized once you pass away. I got news for you, ma. I don't fit that mold. Ben has always treated me normal and everybody who knows me treats me normal. Except you. I don't say anything because I love you and nothing can change that."

Nice's stern visage stared at her. Sally set Yappy on the kitchen floor and began to sob uncontrollably. Nice's countenance softened. He walked over to his mother and helped her stand. He then gave her a tight hug.

"My baby," she said to her son who towered over her. Yappy stood up on her hind legs and began doing her famous dance indicating that she wanted to be included in the hugging.

"Come here, little girl," Nice told Yappy as he swooped her up with one hand.

"That girl wasn't mean to your sister, was she?" Sally asked, regaining her composure.

"No, she likes Yappy." Nice replied.

"I think she was teasing Yappy on Easter."

"No, she wasn't, ma. Yappy was just trying to get her attention, like she does with us to play."

"Did your sister go potty before she came in?"

"Yes, she did."

Sally looked at her son and smiled.

"You are truly nice," Sally stated with sincerity.

Sally headed to her bedroom, followed closely by Yappy.

Nice thought he would pray about the success of his mission.

CHAPTER 32

After church on this Thursday morning, Chelbi and Betty Rondolay drove over to a seamstress located in an older shopping center, situated on the corner of El Camino Real and La Costa Avenue in Carlsbad. Chelbi was going to try on the clothes that Betty bought for her earlier in the week.

The fittings went as planned with the exception of one dress that Betty felt hung too low on the neckline. The seamstress told them that she would make the necessary modifications to correct it to Betty's liking.

Across the street, there was another shopping center with a Starbucks right on the nearest corner. The girls decided to stop for some liquid refreshment. This particular Starbucks had an open patio area and this is where they decided to enjoy their beverage.

"Didn't you think the neck hung down too low on that belted A-line dress, sugar?" Betty inquired.

"Yeah. That's not me," Chelbi relayed.

Chelbi wore dusty rouge, petite, slim-fit, stone washed jeans, a black petite, two-tone layered tee shirt, and an expresso petite, marled faux-suede cardigan. Betty wore gray, Lane Bryant Sophie Birdseye trousers, a sequin Boxy Top shirt, and a black, striped illusion cardigan. Betty also wore her usual rings, three on one hand and two on the other, in addition to a necklace with a small diamond hanging from it.

"Of course it's not, sugar beet. A proper, young lady doesn't advertise those assets. Its best they remain a mystery until you know you're dealing with a gentlemen. That's very important in the South," Betty went on like she was teaching a history lesson and Chelbi seemed to be hanging on her every word.

"They call that *décolletage*," Betty shared, "where the top of the woman's dress or blouse is cut so low, why you can see the outline of her bosoms. I'm sorry, honey," Betty said between sips of her venti Caramel Macchiato, "but that's just trash, pure and simple. It is not for a lady of poise."

Chelbi just nodded and took a sip of her tall Chocolate Chip Frappuccino. Betty was reminded of something and started to chuckle.

"I was thinking about my sister, Roberta Josephine," Betty expressed. "She goes by Bobby Jo. Poor thing. Now, she and I share the same birthday, but ten years apart. She's younger than me. Isn't that all get out?"

Chelbi shook her head affirmatively.

"If you do the math, and back that date up nine months, it was just about daddy's birthday. So, you know he was getting a little bit more than just grits and gravy for a present," Betty told her with a sly nod.

"The boys would always tease my sister," Betty went on. "When God was giving out bosoms, she musta been playin' hooky. Now, I have ample bosoms, but she is an A-cup. A member of the itty, bitty, you-know-what-tee club. When we were kids, they had this TV show, called *Petticoat Junction*. On that show, there were three sisters: Billie Jo, Bobbie Jo and Betty Jo. Their family was involved with a hotel. Anyway, there was a place on the show they always talked about called Hooterville. So, the boys would say to my sister, 'Hey, Bobbie Jo, you should go to Hooterville and get some hooters.' She came home in tears one day and I went down to school and opened up a can of whoop ass on those little pricks and that foolishness stopped."

"Where does your sister live?" Chelbi wondered.

"She still lives in Georgia. She married a podiatrist. Poor soul, he drowned in their backyard pool. But she's got kids and little grandbabies, so she's happy."

"Do you have any children?" Chelbi queried.

"No," Betty shared with a certain degree of melancholy. "It wasn't in God's plan for me." But her attitude changed in a snap. "But now I got you in my life and I know you came to me for a reason."

"Betty, I have to tell you, I am fascinated by everything you say. A week ago, you didn't know me and now you treat me like I'm your daughter."

"I told you the other day, little one, we're family. That's how family treats each other. You're not familiar with the ways of becoming a fine, young lady. I got to help you learn. I need to set an example, so you teach your daughter one day."

Chelbi smiled and took another sip of her drink.

"You know what?" Betty lit up like a Christmas tree. "I got a hankering for ribs. Let's go to Costco. They got the best price on the baby backs. My husband, Bobby, makes a mean barbeque. What do you say, baby chil' (child)?"

"I'm all in," Chelbi exclaimed.

"That's my girl. We'll invite Nice and wear our finest aprons. Deal?"

Betty extended her hand and Chelbi accepted it with a smile.

"You're going to be a Georgia Peach in no time, baby cakes."

There was something about Betty's bossy nature that appealed to Chelbi. It gave her empathy for Nice and what he must have gone through in his life.

CHAPTER 33

Wayne Patterson spent the morning in his Carlsbad Police Headquarters cubicle talking to FBI officials and searching databases for the names, Feardesin and Molech. The FBI was unable to provide any initial assistance, but advised that they would contact Interpol and access worldwide databases. The FBI's initial impression was that the names must be aliases.

Wayne's phone rang and he determined from the Caller ID that it was an internal call.

"This is Patterson," he answered.

"Detective, this is Summers in Dispatch. We just received a call from a woman who was quite adamant that she has information regarding a missing girl. I am going to send you over the transcript of the call."

The Dispatch officer was able to send an e-mail that included a written transcript of the call involving the tip.

Wayne received the e-mail immediately. The woman said that she was renting her apartment to a man who only comes and goes at night. He also covers up his windows. She said she went through his garbage and found something about a girl at Walmart.

The last piece of information regarding Walmart stopped Wayne in his tracks. The parents of Sheila DeLucia, the first abductee, had been on the news asking for the public's assistance in finding their daughter. No information had been put out yet regarding Deborah Wilkinson, the second abductee, who was a Walmart cashier.

Wayne turned on his inner cruise control. He stood from his chair.

"ANDY!" he blurted. "We have to go. NOW!"

Andy stood at his cubicle and looked over the top of the wall at Wayne.

"I'll explain in the car."

With that, both men raced to their unmarked police cruiser to meet with a concerned citizen.

CHAPTER 34

The police cruiser pulled up to a house on Madison Street near Laguna Drive in downtown Carlsbad. The view of the front of the house was blocked by large bushes, some colorful, some dead. The driveway was asphalt that was weathered and neglected.

The two police officers walked up the driveway and the once white, two-story house was in desperate need of a coat of paint. The garage was a stand-alone building located at the left rear corner of the house. They arrived at the front door and Wayne rapped on it.

The door opened slowly. There appeared an elderly Caucasian woman, approximately 80 years old, 5 feet 5 inches, 140 pounds, wearing a worn, blue housedress and a red headwrap that tied at the top, like that worn by Aunt Jemima. Her movements were shaky and she had a cigarette in her hand.

"Hi, Mrs. Vandevere?" Wayne asked. "I'm Detective Patterson and this is Detective Sandoval. We're from the Carlsbad Police. We wanted to talk to you about your tip."

"Oh, good," she answered and then coughed, "come on in."

The two men stepped in, but could not proceed more than six feet into the residence. Mrs. Vandevere was a hoarder. Items lined the floor. Piles of magazines went to the ceiling. The interior looked like a garbage heap. There were empty pizza boxes and various other delivered food items. Clothing was strewn and there were new items still in plastic bags. In one room, there was a TV set on a chair blaring and one chair in front of it. It appeared that Mrs. Vandevere slept on a sleeping bag on one of the piles of items.

"We wanted to talk to you about your tip?" Wayne told her.

"I got this tenant," she began, also interjecting an occasional cough. "Something about the guy ain't right. He comes and goes at night and the windows up there are all covered."

"How do you think he's involved with the missing girl?"

"I like to keep an eye on what's going on around here. I see the guy coming out one night on garbage night and he puts his garbage in the bin I got out on the street. Well, I went out and got his garbage and went through it."

"Do you still have it?" Wayne's voice indicated urgency.

"Yeah," she answered calmly and picked up a plastic grocery bag filled with crushed papers off the floor and handed it to Wayne. "You can take it."

Andy let out with a slight yell that disrupted their conversation. He was shaking his leg and pounding his foot on the floor.

"A cockroach was crawling up my leg," he said in shock.

"They'll do that," Mrs. Vandevere told him. "They like pants."

"Show us what makes you think your tenant is involved with the missing girl?" Wayne inquired.

As Wayne held the plastic bag, Mrs. Vandevere retrieved a single sheet of yellow lined paper from it. On it, it said:

#2 Walmart – cameras in lot. Not there

Also on the sheet, in the same handwriting, but written with a different pen:

Transport trailer – Friday @ Semany
Truck by 10 pm

Wayne examined the paper and looked at Mrs. Vandevere.

"What makes you think this note has something to do with the abducted girl?"

"Look at the back of it."

Wayne turned the page over and in a different, shaky handwriting, was written:

HELP ME!
My name is S

Whoever was writing this note, started the next letter after 'S' and there was a haphazard line, as if the piece of paper was pulled away from the writer.

"That girl who disappeared, isn't her name, Sheila?" Mrs. Vandevere asked.

"Yes, it is," Wayne acknowledged. "What's your tenant's name?"

"His first named is Viktor with a 'k' instead of a 'c.' His last name is either Molech or Molechai."

Wayne knew that they had their man and it pumped him up. "You don't know his last name for sure?" Wayne wondered while Andy was concerned about another roach climbing up his leg.

"He didn't actually rent the place. This company rented it. Paid three months' rent in advance. Told me to just leave the key under the mat."

"What's the name of the company?" Wayne's questions were coming fast and his patience was wearing thin.

She walked a few steps to a high bundle of newspapers, magazines, and books. She went through the top few pieces of paper and pulled out one of them.

"Dorchadas, LLC. I don't have an address."

"What does your tenant look like?" Wayne inquired.

"He's a tall guy, pretty husky, looks like he has curly hair. I've only seen the guy in the dark."

"What kind of car does he drive?"

"Turn that paper I just gave you over." Wayne complied with her request.

On the back of the paper was a combination of six letters and numbers.

"That's his plate number. He drives a brown Toronado. You familiar with that type of car?"

"Yes I am." Wayne stated. "It's an Oldsmobile." Wayne paused for a moment to think of any other information she may be able to provide.

"You think there is going to be a reward?" she asked enthusiastically.

"If there is, you'll get it. If your tenant comes back, I want you to call me," he told her as he handed her his business card. "We'll probably come back with a warrant."

"You can go right now, I'll give you the key."

"Thank you, but we're going to get the warrant," Wayne assured her.

"All right, then. But listen, tell your boys not to break down the door. I'll give'em the key."

"I will make sure they know. Thank you very much, Mrs. Vandevere." Wayne sincerely conveyed.

Both officers went out to the driveway and Wayne began formulating a plan.

"You stay here," he told Andy. "I'll call for an unmarked car to come out and watch the place. This guy will probably come back here tonight and that's when we'll grab him. I'll call in for an APB on the Toronado and I'll run the plates. I'll also see what I can find out about the company that rented this place and our friend, Viktor Molech."

The APB was an 'All-points-bulletin' advising all law enforcement in the County to stop Molech's car if it was seen.

Wayne would also check the Department of Motor Vehicles database to determine who the registered owner of the car was.

Wayne had slightly more than forty-eight hours to find the two abducted girls and less than twenty-four hours to prevent the abduction of the third girl. The endgame had begun.

CHAPTER 35

Wayne raced back to the police station and recruited the assistance of two undercover officers from the Drug Enforcement Unit to assist in the surveillance of Molech's residence. He requested an All-points-bulletin on his ride back for Molech's brown Toronado.

In the office, Wayne determined that the car was a rental from a place called Rental Rats in Van Nuys, California, which is a neighborhood in the central San Fernando Valley region of the City of Los Angeles.

Wayne then enlisted the assistance of two additional detectives to track down information on the rental of the car and search for any information on Viktor Molech.

He further determined that the only physical location he could find with the name 'Semany' was the now-shuttered Semany Wholesale Florists on the corner of Faraday Avenue and Van Allen Way. The Semany Building was only 1.5 miles from the police station.

Wayne decided he wanted to take a look at the building, but was interrupted by the ring of his cell phone. The call was from his wife, Marion.

"Yeah, honey," he answered with a rushed tone.

"You should get over here," Marion told him with deadpan inflection. "As soon as possible."

"What's wrong?"

"Please come now," she replied, her voice on the verge of cracking from tears.

Wayne ended the call, rubbed his forehead, and ran his fingers through his thick, black and gray hair.

He then took off, like a sprinter on fire, to his car.

While racing the twelve miles to the Palomar Medical Center, at speeds in excess of eighty-five miles per hour, Wayne requested a patrol unit to check the Semany Wholesale Flowers building for signs of activity. He wondered if it was a waste of manpower to put the building under 24-hour surveillance or if he had enough probable cause for a warrant.

Time, his home life, and his job were about to squeeze Wayne Patterson. Something was about to crack.

CHAPTER 36

Nice began his day with a list of seventeen locations where he needed to visit to obtain measurements and photographs of broken glass, windows, and sliding glass doors. He would transmit the information to Ben at the shop, who would prepare an estimate and contact the homeowners or businesses with the estimate and then schedule a time for the work to be done.

In addition to this work, Nice had an appointment at 11:45 am with Emil Dobromil, a professor of physics at the University of California at San Diego. Professor Dobromil was noted for his research in quantum physics. He held a PhD degree and was a member of the National Academy of Science. He was also a prior winner of the prestigious Einstein Prize that recognized outstanding accomplishments in the field of gravitational physics. Nice's visit was arranged by his coworker, Diz.

Nice was accompanied by Chelbi, who was now aware of his time travel mission and would offer, at least, emotional support. They parked near Urey Hall and proceeded directly to the seventh floor. The pair located Dr. Dobromil's office and knocked at the door. A voice then responded to the knock.

"Come on in."

Nice and Chelbi entered and the office was a labyrinth of books, magazines, and computer screens. The top of his desk was not visible at all, except for a small area around the telephone.

Dr. Dobromil was sixty-four years old, 5 feet 8 inches tall, 210 pounds with a full head of white hair and a white moustache. He wore brown slacks, with a lighter colored, brown sweater over a light blue, button shirt without a tie.

He met Nice with a smile. He had the look of a kindly, old grandfather.

"Can I help you?" the professor asked.

"Dr. Dobromil, my name is Nicean Bevilacqua, I'm Diz's friend."

"Oh, yeah, yeah," he was now recalling, "How are you, Nice?"

"I'm fine. Peace be with you. This is my friend, Chelbi." He hung on to the last syllable of her name because he realized that he did not know her last name.

"Gorringe." Chelbi supplemented Nice's introduction.

"I'm pleased to meet both of you. We are going to go right down the hall to a conference room. Follow me."

They followed him two doors down to a room that contained a rectangular metal table with eight chairs and a whiteboard on one of the walls. The room had a partial view of the ocean and parking lot below. Nice and Chelbi sat with their backs to the windowed wall and Dr. Dobromil sat at the head of the table.

"So, how's my friend, Diz?" the professor asked.

"He's doing well," Nice responded.

"He's a good man. Smart guy, too. We wanted him to be a professor down here, but he wasn't interested. You must work at a pretty great place."

"It is a great place to work," Nice acknowledged.

"How many years you been there?" Dr. Dobromil asked.

"Four, full-time. Three years part-time before that."

"So, how can I help you?"

"I really have two questions for you. I tried to research them, but found it very confusing. The first question I have is, do you know if time travel is possible?"

"Well, your good friend, Diz, sent you to the right guy. I did my doctorate dissertation on general relativity and various hybrid theories involving quantum gravity."

Nice and Chelbi both continued to smile at him, but had no idea what he was talking about.

"To answer your question: In theory – yes; in practice – no. Time travel is the stuff of textbooks and movies."

"You said in theory, it is possible. Any chance the government may have like a secret time machine that no one knows about?"

"That's possible, but then I wouldn't know about it, because it was secret." Nice looked confused. "Look, I don't think you would benefit from a long, scientific explanation. A simple, factual scenario for this situation is that if there were time machines, why don't we have any evidence in all of recorded history of a person coming back in time? There may be some mental cases out there who think they have, but science is always able to debunk them."

"You have to admit, there are a lot of unexplained events that have occurred. Maybe a time machine was involved with them?" Nice suggested.

"Maybe. But I'm a scientist who likes to think there's more to life than science. I think you and Diz would agree. This school is one of the best educational institutions in the country and I would love to tell you that we have a machine in the back that can send you to 1492. But I can't. I'm sorry."

"Okay," Nice told him with a crestfallen smile. "Thank you for your time, Doctor."

They both stood and exchanged handshakes.

"You can come and see me any time," the Doctor shared with Nice. "And say 'Hello' to Diz for me."

"I will."

Nice was quiet as they left the building and walked to his truck. Before he started the truck, he had a comment for Chelbi.

"You probably think I'm a real fool." As he spoke, he just looked forward.

"No! Not at all. I don't know anyone who would take the actions you have to try to save Jesus," Chelbi retorted unequivocally.

"I bet there are a couple of them in mental institutions who said they were going to do it."

"If they have faith like you, then they're in the wrong place."

Nice appreciated her comment and looked at her with a smile.

"You want to come with me for the rest of my stops today?" he wondered.

"Yeah," she replied and, after a moment, added, "and my last name is Gorringe!"

"Sorry about that. Nobody ever told me."

"You *could* ask."

As they drove back to Carlsbad, north on the Interstate 5 freeway, Nice was saddened that his plan was a complete and utter failure. He was glad that he told no one but Chelbi, and he knew that the implosion of his plan would haunt him. Nice believed that the person he loved the most, he had let down the most.

CHAPTER 37

While en route to the Palomar Medical Center, Wayne Patterson received word from one of the patrol units that there was no activity at the Semany Wholesale Flowers building and all the doors were secured. Wayne thanked the men for checking it and turned his attention to the condition of his daughter.

He had made this trip so many times that the process of driving to the hospital was a mechanical function, devoid of conscious thought. He parked close to a hospital entrance door in a short term, parking space.

Wayne dashed to the elevator and wished he could make it move faster for his ride to the sixth floor. When the doors opened, he scurried with heightened urgency to his daughter's room.

Upon entering, he saw that she was alone, but she was now connected to a medical ventilator, complete with a mask that covered her nose and mouth. This ventilator used a computer algorithm to determine the amount of compression to force air, tempered with oxygen, into her lungs. Her lungs would then contract automatically. This device was different from a respirator that merely filters inhaled air.

Wayne walked up to the right side of the bed and took Joy's left hand with his left hand and gently rubbed her forehead with his right hand. Before long, Marion and a doctor appeared at the doorway.

"Wayne," Marion spoke up to get his attention. "This is Doctor Harron. He's in charge of oncology here at the hospital."

Dr. Harron was thirty-eight years old, 6 feet 1 inch tall, and weighed 190 pounds. He wore glasses and had brown, balding hair. He wore a white lab coat, with his name sewn in red over the left pocket. His shirt was white and his tie was striped in blue and gold.

Wayne turned to confront the doctor.

"Doctor, why is my daughter on a respirator?" he asked, with his voice evidencing a growing anger.

"It's a ventilator, sir. It helps your daughter breathe."

"Isn't that used when someone is brain dead?"

"Not necessarily, sir. It's serving the function we need for her right now and that is to assist her with her breathing."

"Wayne," Marion interjected, "I was just having a conversation with the doctor. The hospital feels that it would be best to send Joy home with hospice care."

"WHAT!" Wayne was incredulous. "The hospital feels, since when does a hospital feel anything? So, you're giving up on her?" He pointed the question to Dr. Harron. "You decided that it's time for her to die?"

"Mr. Patterson," now the doctor's voice was slightly raised. "Your daughter coded today. She flatlined. We had to give her a shot of epinephrine directly into her heart. If a crash cart wasn't close by, you would be planning her funeral right now. And if you think it doesn't tear me up inside to watch someone like your daughter die so painfully slow, you are gravely mistaken. I became a doctor to save people, not kill them. The radiation and the chemotherapy are killing your daughter. The treatment is worse than the disease. So, we are done. My goal now is to make her comfortable. She should be strong enough in a few days to go home."

Wayne heard what was said and it registered with him, but he didn't want to hear it. He was suddenly sullen and morose. He turned to his daughter and resumed holding her hand and rubbing her forehead.

Wayne knew that the fate of his daughter was now sealed. At this moment, he had no interest in abducted girls, a warehouse, or surveillance. All he could do was wonder about what kind of a God could allow this?

CHAPTER 38

Wayne returned to work the next morning and upon his arrival, there was a phone message waiting for him on his desk. The message was from Shelley Palmer, the roommate of Deborah Wilkinson, the second girl to be abducted. He would return this call to start his day.

He removed his sport coat and placed it on the back of his chair. He called over to his partner at a nearby cubicle, but there was no response. Wayne dialed Shelley's number. She answered on the third ring.

"Hello."

"Hello, Shelley. This is Detective Patterson of the Carlsbad Police, I was returning your call."

"Thanks for calling, Detective. I wanted to check in to see if you heard anything? I was wondering if I should call her mother."

"We're following every lead. I am going to find her," Wayne's voice was certain. The question in his mind was whether or not she would be alive.

"All right, then," Shelley told him. "The only person who called looking for her was her nun friend and I didn't want to say anything until you said . . ."

Wayne suddenly cut her off.

"Who did you say called for her?"

"Oh, she knows this nun and I know they talk on a regular basis. Deborah told me once that she might even join them."

Wayne remembered that when the parents of Sheila DeLucia, the first abductee, were at the police station, the mother said that Sheila was thinking about becoming a nun.

"What's her name?" Wayne's voice pulsed with urgency.

"Who?" Shelley asked.

"The nun that called."

"Sister Mary O'Dell. You want her number?"

"Yes, please."

Shelley shared the number with Wayne and he thanked her for calling. Wayne immediately dialed the number.

He learned that the number was for the Carmelite Monastery located in the Mission Valley area of San Diego. When Wayne dialed Sister O'Dell's extension, a recorded message said she was unavailable. He attempted to contact her via other extensions, but received the same recorded message.

Wayne hung up the phone and stood, while grabbing his coat. He wanted to talk to Sister O'Dell now and he was going to find her. Before leaving, he wanted to speak to his partner for an update on the surveillance. He found Andy Sandoval in the hallway, speaking with another officer.

"Anything happen with the surveillance?" Wayne asked, referring to the surveillance of Molech's apartment.

"No, he never came back," Andy told him."

Wayne shook his head in disbelief.

"What about the car?" he posed a second inquiry.

"Nothing."

"All right," Wayne declared. "I'm going down to San Diego to talk to a nun. Both of the girls were interested in becoming nuns. This could be their connection."

"You want me to go with you?" Andy asked.

"I'd rather you stay here in case Molech surfaces or they find his car. If they do, you start hammering away on him."

"Wayne, listen. A black and white unit brought in a guy who says he knows you and he wants to talk."

"What's his name?"

"Patricio Lopez. He's from San Marcos."

Wayne was shaking his head affirmatively as Andy spoke.

"I know him. Goes by 'Treese.' What did they pick him up for?" Wayne wondered.

Treese was the man who sold the machine gun to Nice.

"Ran a light," Andy revealed. "A girl was in the car with him acting all twitchy. She had a bag of Meth in her purse. This guy, Patricio, is on paper for a weapons violation. The girl in the car has a felony record."

Treese was on parole or 'on paper' for a conviction dealing with the sale of guns. As a parolee, he is prohibited from associating with known felons.

"Where is he?"

Andy directed Wayne to an interrogation room where Treese was sitting. Treese wore a black t-shirt and black jeans.

"Treese," Wayne exclaimed as he entered the room and stood, looking at him across the table. "It's been a long time. How are you?"

"I've been better," Treese responded.

"What can I do for you?" Wayne asked.

"Look, Detective Wayne, I just met that girl last night. I didn't know she had a record and I would have never let her in my car if I knew she was holding. You gotta help me out. I don't want to go back to the joint."

"Treese, you know how we operate around her. The commodity is information. What do you have for me?"

Treese looked at Wayne for a moment and thought about what he was going to say.

"This guy came to my shop the other day. He wanted to buy a machine gun."

"If the guy is from anyplace, other than Carlsbad, I'm not interested."

"This guy said he was from Carlsbad."

"Did you sell him a machine gun?"

"Detective Wayne, I'm trying to get out of trouble, not dig the hole deeper."

"Did the guy say what he wanted it for?"

"No. But he said he wanted it loud."

"You got a name?" Wayne inquired.

"It was an odd name." Treese struggled to remember. "He said it fast."

Wayne walked toward the door.

"When you got something for me, I'll see what I can do for you."

As Wayne reached for the door handle, Treese blurted the name out.

"Nice. The guy's name was Nice."

The statement stopped Wayne in his tracks. He turned back to Treese.

"What did he look like?"

"Tall guy. Blond hair. Good build. Real polite. And he was good with the gun."

The wheels in Wayne's mind were smoking. He immediately thought about Nice's outburst in church on Good Friday.

Wayne opened the door and called a uniformed officer over to the doorway.

"Let him go," Wayne told the officer, referring to Treese.

"Thanks, Detective Wayne."

Wayne didn't need this new problem involving Nice, but he had to deal with it now. He knew Nice wanted people to listen and perhaps Nice thought the machine gun was the way to do it.

CHAPTER 39

When Nice arrived at Ben's Glassworks this morning, Ben and Chelbi were there waiting. Nice wore his normal uniform, which consisted of blue Dickies pants and a light blue, Ben's Glassworks t-shirt. Chelbi wore a blue and white flannel shirt, jean skirt, and a t-shirt that simply said, in cursive writing, "THAT'S HOW I ROLL!" Ben wore a light blue button shirt with the Ben's Glassworks logo over the right pocket.

"Chelbi, Ben, peace be with you both," Nice addressed them with his usual salutation. "Where's Diz and Lozo?"

"Lozo's out on a job and Diz had a doctor's appointment."

"How's the day look, Ben?" Nice wondered.

"Busy. I understand Chelbi helped you out yesterday?"

"She did. I think she did a good job."

Ben then turned to her. "Ask him."

"I was wondering if I could go with you today?" she asked. "I want to learn a little more about the glass business."

"What do you think, Ben?" Nice asked.

"It's up to you," Ben replied. "I don't care as long as the work gets done."

"It's fine with me as long as you stay focused and there's no drama," Nice explained.

"There won't be," Chelbi assured him.

"All right." Nice then turned to Ben. "What are we doing today?"

"Estimates," Ben declared bluntly. "I've got a list of sixteen places you have to visit. It's the usual. Sizes, photographs, and the type of glass. Also, make a note if you think you can handle the install."

"Do you want us to send them to you for each place as we're done?"

"Might as well. This way we'll have two sets in case I screw it up on the computer."

"It's not you, Ben. It's the computer that screws it up," Nice informed him with a smile.

"I wish," Ben confessed. "Oh, I almost forgot."

Ben sauntered as quickly as he could into the office and came back with a padlock key in hand.

"One of the places you have to go to is the old Semany Wholesale building. It's on the corner of Faraday and Van Allen, near that 7-Eleven we go to every once in a while. They have a skylight that's broken. So, you're going to have to get on the roof," Ben advised. "On the side of the building, there's a ladder permanently secured to it that goes all the way to the top. At the bottom, there's a six and a half foot galvanized, steel door that covers it. This is the key to unlock the padlock on the door."

As Ben spoke the last sentence, he handed the key to Nice.

"On that job, in addition to the measurements and pictures, see if you can find the manufacturer's name and the model number. The skylight should open, but I don't know how old it is. So, bring some tools with you. See if you can bring a piece of the glass back.

It should be Plexiglas and it's probably domed. I need to find out if we can order the piece or if it is something we can fabricate here in the shop. Okay?"

"No problem," Nice declared.

"If you have any questions while you're up there, call me."

"Will do," Nice informed him with a smile.

"Hey, if you guys are going to lunch," Ben was quick to add, "Call me. My treat."

"You got it, my friend," Nice answered, retaining his wide smile.

Nice and Chelbi headed out for what began as a normal work day. The day would end much differently than it began and lives would be changed forever.

CHAPTER 40

The Carmelite Monastery was located approximately thirty-three miles from the Carlsbad Police Department on Hawley Boulevard in the Mission Valley section of San Diego. Wayne drove at speeds in excess of eighty miles per hour for most of the ride there and would occasionally put on his unmarked cruiser's lights in order to get traffic to move. He was at the Monastery within thirty minutes.

Wayne located the business office and asked for Sister Mary O'Dell. At the time, Sister O'Dell was in the process of caring for an elderly sister. While Wayne nervously waited for Sister O'Dell, he stepped into the hallway and called his partner, Andy Sandoval, and told him to begin the paperwork for a warrant to search the Semany Wholesale Flowers building. Wayne shared with Andy all the various information that he wanted in the warrant and asked him to speed it up, so they could conduct the search this afternoon.

"Anything on Molech?" Wayne wondered.

"Zip. The guys are just sitting out there. Should I call them back or try to get a warrant for the apartment?" Andy inquired.

"Leave them there. Let's focus on the warehouse. Tell Ross Hardiman to have his SWAT guys ready for a tactical response."

Just then, Sister O'Dell appeared. She was 5 feet 4 inches tall, 125 pounds, wearing her habit, which consisted of a brown tunic, with a brown scapular running the full length of the tunic like an apron. A rosary hung from her woolen belt. On her head was a white coif, secured by a white wimple and black veil. You could see her white hair around the edge of the wimple and she wore large, rimless glasses.

"Detective Patterson?" she posed her inquiry.

"I have to go," he said to Andy and turned his attention to the nun. "Hello, Sister. It's nice to meet you."

"As it is with me, sir. I hope you're having a blessed day. How can I be of assistance to you?"

Wayne realized that she had a tinge of an accent, but it was almost indiscernible.

"I understand, Sister, that you know Deborah Wilkinson of Carlsbad."

"Yes, I do. She's a lovely, young girl," Sister O'Dell voiced.

"Well, she's missing and I'm trying to find her."

"Oh no, I just spoke to her over the weekend. Do you think she'll be all right?"

"I hope so. May I ask: Did you happen to know another young girl from Carlsbad, named Sheila DeLucia?"

"Don't tell me something happened to her?" The nun's shock was evident.

"She's missing also," Wayne's voice echoed desperation.

"I'll alert the other nuns. We'll commence a Rosary immediately. What about Darlene?"

Wayne's interest was now off the chart.

"Tell me about Darlene?" Wayne's voice screamed exigency.

"Our ranks as nuns continue to diminish. You know the harvest is great and the laborers are few. We felt so blessed to have three young ladies from Carlsbad all express an interest in joining our order. They were an answer to our prayers. I have been speaking to all three of them weekly over the past year."

"I need Darlene's number and address," Wayne told her.

"I'll get it for you," Sister O'Dell moved swiftly to the Monastery Office.

"Sister, do you happen to know a man named Feardesin?"

Sister O'Dell stopped suddenly and the blood drained from her face.

"What was that name again, sir?" She spoke slowly and deliberately.

"Feardesin. Do you know somebody with that name?"

"I do," she uttered without emotion.

"Where do you know that name from?"

"The Bible."

"Explain to me what you mean, Sister."

"My parents were born here in America, but my grandparents were from the 'old sod.' Ireland. County Cork. So, their first language was the Irish Gaelic. My grandmother was always quoting Scripture in Gaelic and telling my mother to translate. Feardesin or *fear de sin* means, 'man of sin.' Second Thessalonians, Chapter two, verses three and four. That's one of the names in the Bible for the Devil."

Wayne stared at her as if they were both in suspended animation. Time had stopped for that moment while Wayne tried to comprehend what he just heard. He refocused.

"I need that information on Darlene."

Sister O'Dell immediately proceeded to retrieve it.

Wayne raced back to Carlsbad as if he was in a high-speed pursuit. As soon as he started the car, he called his partner, Andy Sandoval. Andy answered his phone on the first ring.

"Sandoval speaking," he answered without conscious thought.

"Andy," Wayne spoke with frenetic energy. "The third girl is Darlene Evans. She lives with her parents at 1102 Coneflower Drive. Send a black and white unit over there now. Put an APB out on her car. Find out what her parents drive. Put an APB out on their car. I'm going to keep trying to call her. Did you finish the warrant?"

"Almost done."

"Okay. Let's see if we can get to this girl before Molech does. Feardesin is an alias. This whole thing might have something to do with a satanic ritual. We have to check out that angle. I'll keep trying to call this girl."

Wayne was in motion as he dialed Darlene's phone number. It was 11:00 am.

Meanwhile, at Darlene's house, she had just entered her garage and opened the overhead door. She wheeled her 11-speed, Nashbar CR4 road bike out to commence her daily eleven mile trek to Double Peak Park in San Marcos, a city located to the east of Carlsbad.

Darlene pressed a code on a keypad that allowed the overhead door to close. As she was entering the code, she could hear the phone ringing in her house.

It was Detective Wayne Patterson. Darlene decided to let the answering machine pick it up.

CHAPTER 41

Darlene Evans was a triathlete. The temperate weather of Carlsbad was so ideal that many triathletes moved there just to take advantage of it. As part of her exercise regimen, Darlene would bicycle four days a week to the Double Peak Park located eleven miles away in San Marcos, California, a city located immediately to the east of Carlsbad.

Darlene was 23 years old, 5 feet 6 inches tall, 128 pounds, with brown, shoulder-length hair. She was not fond of makeup, and she did not need it. She had a cuteness that was backed up by the strength of an iron woman.

She enjoyed the long passages of solitude brought forth by her physical training and the only other place she found that, outside of exercising, was from going to church and reading her Bible.

On this day, Darlene wore a yellow, Performance Flow Wind Jacket, black, Elite shorts, blue and black Giro Sica MTB shoes, a Bell Star Pro Race helmet, and metallic red Podium Fototec sunglasses. Her jacket contained pockets that allowed her to carry water and a quick snack, if she desired.

Her bicycle was an 11-speed, Ultegra Nashbar, CR4 carbon road bike. This lightweight bike was extremely fast, responsive and handled serious uphill climbs well.

Her trek to the Double Peak Park was mostly urban roads that were shared with traffic. Once she reached Double Peak Road in San Marcos, traffic would become very light, which she appreciated during her assent to the top of the peak. This 1.1 mile stretch of her journey was always the most challenging due to its uphill climb.

Double Peak Park is located approximately 1644 feet above sea level in the Cerro de las Posas Mountains. The spectacular view allows visitors to see the Pacific Ocean, located twelve miles away.

One of Molech's men had Darlene's house under surveillance and called Molech to advise that she had begun her bicycle journey.

Inside the Semany Flowers Warehouse, Molech dialed a number and waited for an answer.

"Yeah," a voice responded.

"Make the call," Molech ordered. He then turned to another man in the room. "Raise the volume on the scanner."

Molech and his men were listening to the radio traffic of the Carlsbad Police on a police scanner.

The man that Molech told to make a call was standing in front of a telephone company switching station, located near the street, that was within one block of the Carlsbad High School located on Monroe Street in northern Carlsbad. The man wore a yellow hard hat and a yellow, fluorescent vest. He connected a handheld telephone device within the switching station and dialed three numbers. The call was quickly answered.

"Nine-one-one. What is your emergency?"

A voice quietly responded, without emotion.

"There is a bomb inside locker 1802 at Carlsbad High School. It's set to go off in twenty minutes. There are two students who plan to open fire on the other students as they are being evacuated. Tick tock. Tick tock."

He then disconnected the call.

Within thirty seconds, the radio traffic on the scanner went wild. All available units that were not at an active crime scene, including the unit periodically checking the Semany Warehouse and the men watching Molech's apartment, were ordered to the high school.

Molech and two other men entered the white van that was used to abduct Deborah Wilkinson, the second victim. Another man got into a gray, Ford Taurus, while still another man was going to drive a black, Chevrolet pickup truck.

Molech had commenced the execution of his plan.

CHAPTER 42

Nice and Chelbi had looked at six locations for window repairs within ninety minutes. Theresa, Ben's wife, would always set up the estimate jobs in a geographic order, so Nice would not be traveling all over the San Diego County.

The last job they looked at was in San Marcos and Nice was driving back to the Carlsbad area.

"What do you like for lunch?" Nice inquired.

"I don't care. I'm pretty easy going," Chelbi responded.

"Do you like burgers?"

"They're okay," she answered with a smile.

"Your grandfather really likes them. So, that's where we're going to go. Do you have a favorite kind of burger place?"

"In Kansas, I really like Hardees. I love the waffle-cut French fries. Can we go there?"

"I don't think we have a Hardees here in Carlsbad," Nice informed her.

"I saw one when I was driving around with Betty. It had a big star in the front."

"Big star?" Nice wondered. Then came a moment of realization. "Carl's Junior. It must be Carl's Junior."

"We call them Hardees in Kansas."

"I didn't know that," Nice replied, grateful for that piece of information. "Listen, why don't we get that Semany Wholesale job out of the way and then we'll go pick up some food at Carl's Junior and bring it back to the shop."

"You're driving," Chelbi said. "Do you think we could stop somewhere, so I could go to the bathroom?"

"Yeah, there's a 7-Eleven right next to the Semany Wholesale."

Nice and Chelbi did not know it, but they were about to visit their last job of the day.

CHAPTER 43

In less than twenty minutes from the time she left her house, Darlene Evans turned onto Double Peak Drive for the last 1.1 miles to the Double Peak Park parking lot. The road starts out fairly level and then becomes challenging as the road ascends to the top of the peak.

Darlene liked to increase her speed before the road began its steep ascent.

Shortly after Darlene turned onto this road, a gray, Ford Taurus, a white, Dodge van, and a black, Chevy pickup truck followed her path. The vehicles quickly caught up to Darlene with the gray Taurus driving slightly ahead of her, the white van keeping pace with the bicycle, and the black pickup following behind her.

Inside the back of the van, Molech was down on one knee next to the sliding side door of the windowless vehicle. He motioned for one of the other men to hand him something and he was given a Barnett C5 crossbow that was cocked and loaded with a twenty-two inch carbon arrow. The body of the crossbow looked like a tactical rifle and it had a sighting system to enhance the shooter's accuracy.

Molech took the crossbow and placed it against his shoulder, then waved to the man who handed him the crossbow to prepare to open the sliding door of the van.

Darlene always tried not to focus on the activity of the vehicles during her ride as long as they gave her enough room on the side of the road.

Inside the van, Molech kneeled ready to fire.

"We're coming up on the hill," the driver said.

Molech looked at the man holding the door handle to the sliding door and nodded.

The door was pulled open immediately and within one second, Molech aimed at the front fork of Darlene's bicycle and fired. The arrow flew between the two front forks and became locked by the spokes of the front tire slamming into it. The entire front tire froze as if the brakes were slammed on. The back of the bike lifted up as it pivoted over the front tire.

Darlene immediately switched into survival mode and let go of the handlebars and prepared to hit the ground and roll. She could not clear her body from the bike quick enough and it slammed down onto her right leg.

The three vehicles stopped immediately. The first and third vehicles were serving to block sight of what was going on next to the van.

One of the men jumped out of the van and picked the bicycle up off Darlene and threw it inside the van. Another man from the van went to Darlene to pick her up by her left arm. When she stood, she broke his grip and immediately took a boxing position. One man went in to grab her and she hit him with a left hook and then a right hook, connecting with his face both times and he backed away from her.

She then turned to focus on the other man. Her leg was throbbing with pain, so running was not an option. A voice then seemed to stop the action.

"Get in the van," Molech commanded and both of his compatriots complied.

Darlene turned to Molech and resumed her fighting stance.

Molech walked up to her and she took a swing at his face. He put up his left hand to block her punch and with his right hand, he immediately brought the jet injector vaccine gun filled with the paralyzing agent, vecuronium bromide, to her neck and fired. She pulled away quickly and wondered what he had done. The drug began to take effect almost immediately.

Molech's men grabbed Darlene and placed her in the back of the van. The sliding door of the van closed and any trace of Darlene had vanished.

Molech's assignment was now complete. All that was left was for him to turn over the three women to Feardesin's representative.

CHAPTER 44

Nice parked the Ben's Glassworks, white, Ford, pickup truck on Van Allen Way, adjacent to the east side of the Semany Warehouse building. The parking to the east contained a strip shopping center that included, among other things, a food court, dental office, and nail salon. A 7-Eleven gas station sat in the corner of that parking lot at Faraday Avenue and Van Allen Way.

"I'm going to see if I can use the bathroom in the 7-Eleven," Chelbi announced.

"Okay," Nice told her as he opened his door. Then he turned back to her. "Are you going to be okay?"

"Yeah. I can go to the bathroom by myself. I'm a big girl," Chelbi informed him sarcastically, yet appreciated his concern. "Why, did you want to come with me?"

"No. But if you wanted me to go, I would."

"I'll be fine," she assured him.

"Here," Nice said handing her the keys to the truck.

"Why are you giving these to me?"

"When you're with a young lady and you know that you're going to be separated, you should make sure that she has a ride, in case something happens."

Chelbi looked at him with a coy smirk.

"That sounds like Ben talking," she mused.

"Well, this sounds like Nice listening," Nice declared.

They both exited the truck and Nice grabbed his Bible. Chelbi crossed the street while Nice selected several tools from a toolbox in the back of the truck. He placed them, with his Bible, into a worn, leather bag that he used to tote tools when he does not need the entire tool box. The leather bag had a long strap that allowed him to put the bag over his shoulder to carry it.

Nice saw the ladder to the roof and walked over to it immediately. He unlocked the six and a half foot galvanized, steel door that covered the bottom of the ladder and ascended the twenty feet to mount the roof.

The roof was flat and the floor of it consisted mostly of hardened tar, mopped around the various ducts and air conditioning units. At the southern end of the building, in the center of the garage area was the lone skylight.

Around the base of the skylight, the hardened tar ran around the perimeter on the raised portion of it. The glass portion of it was domed and appeared to be made of Plexiglas. In the center of the domed glass was a smashed hole, approximately the size of a bowling ball. Nice took a pliers and broke off a small piece of one of the jagged edges to bring back to the shop as Ben had requested.

Before measuring it, he took out his cell phone to obtain several photos.

"Hey, let me do that," a voice uttered. Chelbi had made her way to the top of the roof. "The bathroom over there was out of order."

Nice handed the phone to Chelbi and he took out a measuring tape from his bag. The skylight measured exactly eight feet by four feet. Nice knew that he also had to obtain the manufacturer's name and the model number.

There was a hinge that ran along one of the eight foot sides of the skylight and fourteen screws held the other three sides in place. Nice began to loosen the tar and removed the screws.

Years of inactivity made the cover, at first, difficult to move. Nice opened it and placed his head inside the opening to look for the product information. Chelbi also got on her knees to search and decided to take a few photos.

Nice and Chelbi were not paying attention to each other and bumped their heads. At that moment, Chelbi lost her grip on the cell phone and it fell to the floor of the darkened garage twenty feet below. It appeared that the back of the phone popped off.

They both raised their heads slowly and looked at each other. Nice smiled at her and they both chuckled.

"Sorry about that," Chelbi confessed.

"That's all right," Nice answered to assuage her concerns. "Let's see what we can do here."

Nice looked around and then looked in his tool bag. In the tool bag was a safety harness, a vertical rope with lanyards, and gloves. Nice was supposed to put these items back on the shelf at the shop on the day he went with Diz, but that day he was in a hurry to meet Treese to buy the machine gun.

"Hey, are you in the mood for a little adventure?"

"I'm there," Chelbi declared.

"You put this safety harness on and I'll lower you to the floor of the garage to get the phone."

"Sounds like a plan."

Chelbi put the harness on quickly and then sat on the edge of the open skylight. Nice made sure the rope was connected to the safety harness and he put on the heavy cloth gloves. Before she slowly pushed off the edge, she had one more comment.

"I trust you."

Nice responded to her with a wink.

Chelbi pushed slowly off the ledge of the skylight and Nice found it quite easy to lower her to the floor. She picked up the phone and tried to put it together on the spot.

"Chelbi, don't worry about it," Nice informed her as his voice echoed throughout the garage.

"Nice, I'm going to see if they have a bathroom in here," she told him and unhooked her lanyard from the safety harness. She slipped out of the harness quickly and began her search for a ladies room.

Nice continued to check the perimeter of the skylight for model information. Chelbi was about to make a discovery.

CHAPTER 45

As Wayne Patterson continued to move at speeds of eighty-five to ninety miles per hour in his unmarked Carlsbad Police cruiser up the Interstate 5 freeway, he called his partner, Andy Sandoval.

"Andy, what's going on with the warrant for the warehouse?" Wayne quizzed.

"Just waiting on a signature. Have you been listening to the radio?" Andy's voice pulsed concern.

"I called the Chief and told him that the school call was a decoy," Wayne advised. "So everybody would be in that part of the city while they're grabbing Darlene Evans somewhere else. Probably toward Encinitas or San Marcos."

"You might be onto something. I spoke to Darlene's mother. Darlene takes a daily bike ride to Double Peak Park in San Marcos. It's about eleven miles each way from her house near Poinsettia Park."

"They must have her by now," Wayne exclaimed with a tone of futility. "Listen carefully, Andy. I want a black and white unit to back us up and I also want a SWAT team to mount up to provide backup. That place is pretty big."

"We can't get a SWAT team. We are not going to be able to pull them off the high school."

"Andy, I told you it was a decoy."

"Wayne, they found a bomb."

"Was it an actual ordinance?"

Wayne wondered if they found a live bomb.

"I don't know," Andy told him. "The County bomb squad is there now. One other thing that didn't go out over the radio: The caller said that two students were going to open fire on the other students during the evacuation."

Wayne's frustration level continued to escalate.

"Has anybody been shot yet?" Wayne demanded an answer.

"No."

"I will get the SWAT team," Wayne told him while trying to hold back his vitriolic rage. "Get the warrant and the black and white unit and meet me at the warehouse as soon as you can."

Wayne ended the call fearful of the kidnapper's next move now that all three girls were in their possession.

CHAPTER 46

Ten minutes earlier, Molech and his caravan of three vehicles calmly drove the speed limit for the nearly ten miles on their way to the Semany Warehouse. Darlene Evans lay passed out on the floor of the van being watched by two of Molech's henchmen, while Molech sat in the passenger seat.

At that moment, Molech's cell phone came to life. He retrieved it and looked at the number on the Caller ID. He recognized the number.

"Yes," he answered.

"Mr. Molech? It's Mr. Feardesin. I trust your work is completed."

"It's done," Molech responded in his slow, monotone voice. "Is the transport vehicle on its way?"

"Oh, there's been a change in plans," Feardesin calmly advised with pride. "When you get back to the warehouse, I want you to kill them all."

"WHAT!" Molech's voice flared with emotion.

"Kill them. Then get out. Do you understand me?" Feardesin's voice was austere and resolute.

"What about my money?" Molech demanded.

"You completed the assignment, you will get paid. One additional thing: A young man is coming to save them. Kill him, too."

"When do I get my money?" Molech pressed him.

"WHENEVER I PLEASE!" Feardesin screamed into the phone. His voice came across the phone line like it was in stereo. "Now, do what you're told!" With that, Feardesin ended the call.

Molech closed his flip phone and looked over his shoulder at Darlene Evan's motionless body. He wondered what Feardesin's motive was in all this. Then, he realized that it was better not to have an opinion.

CHAPTER 47

Chelbi entered the office portion of the warehouse in search of the ladies room. She found it at the end of a corridor on the eastern side of the building. It was dark in the corridor and she proceeded slowly.

She pushed the door open and the creak of the door hinges filled the air. The room was dark and she reached her hand along the wall to find the light switch. She flicked it and as the light flooded the room, Chelbi let out a gasp.

Sheila DeLucia and Deborah Wilkinson were restrained with chains on the floor. Their mouths were covered with duct tape. Chelbi ran over to Deborah and took the duct tape off her mouth.

"Help us, please," Deborah pleaded with a total lack of energy. "They keep us drugged."

"I'm gonna get my friend, he'll get you out of here," Chelbi told Deborah as she removed the duct tape from Sheila's mouth.

Chelbi looked at the chains and saw they were clasped on with a padlock.

"I'll be right back," she told them and raced out screaming. "NICE! NICE!"

Nice heard Chelbi's screams and immediately connected the vertical rope to a section of the closest air conditioning unit. He made sure the rope was taut and then sat on the rim of the skylight. He lowered himself down to the floor as quickly as he could by allowing the rope to slip through his gloved hands. The first thing he saw was Molech's Toronado parked at the far end of the garage.

Chelbi continued to scream his name as she ran up to him.

"There're two girls in the bathroom. They're chained up on the floor. They said somebody is keeping them drugged."

"Show me," Nice requested with urgency as they both darted back to the bathroom.

Nice saw the girls and he was horrified.

"Chelbi, see if the phone works," Nice uttered as fast as he could speak. "Call nine-one-one. If the phone's not working go back to the 7-Eleven and call nine-one-one."

Nice returned to the ladies bathroom to see if he could remove the chains that wrapped them. He knew he could carry them out if the chains were not removed.

"I'm going to stand you up," he told Sheila. Nice put her on her feet. "I'm going to stand you up, too," he advised Deborah and placed her on her feet.

These girls were approximately the same height. Nice bent down and placed each of his shoulders against one of the girl's waists. He put his arms around their waists to secure them and lifted. Both girls were now in the air on Nice's shoulders.

As Nice was pulling the girls out, Chelbi determined that the phone would not turn on. She had to go to the 7-Eleven. In the garage, she looked for an exit door. There were two man doors on the eastern side of the garage, the side closest to the 7-Eleven. She sprinted to both of them, but they were bolted on the inside.

Chelbi then saw a sign on the wall, above a plunger switch, that said 'Overhead Door.' She pushed the button for the door and it started to raise, then abruptly started to lower. When the door was down, she pushed the button again. She began to bolt toward the overhead door when she saw the reason it retracted.

There were the three vehicles from Molech's motorcade. She dashed to the other side of the garage.

"Did you see that?" the driver of the van said to Molech as the vehicles continued to enter the building. "It looked like a little kid."

The van, truck, and car entered the darkened garage and the overhead door was lowered. The men exited the vehicles.

"Go get that little kid," Molech commanded. Two of the men took off after Chelbi.

Chelbi was pushing against one of the doors on the western side of the building when she was grabbed by one of the men and carried back to Molech. In the interim, Molech sent one of his men into the office to get something for him.

"What are you doing in here?" Molech asked Chelbi.

"Fixing the skylight," she responded pointing up to it in the roof.

"How are you fixing it from down here?" he again asked.

"I dropped my phone. I was able to get down here on that rope. I was opening up the door to get out."

Outside, Detective Wayne Patterson pulled into the parking lot and made a quick sweep around the warehouse in his cruiser. He parked near one of the doors on the western side of the building. Wayne was waiting for his partner, the backup officers, and the SWAT team.

Molech looked at Chelbi and considered her fate. As he was doing this, Nice lumbered into the warehouse garage carrying both girls. Nice locked eyes with Molech.

"Well, well," Molech announced. "What do we have here? Did you come to fix the skylight also?"

"I did," Nice answered.

"Put them down," Molech demanded.

Nice did not respond.

Outside, Detective Andy Sandoval and a black and white unit arrived with two officers.

"He could snap her neck pretty easy," Molech asserted, referring to the man holding Chelbi.

Nice bent forward and set the two girls down on their feet. Both girls began to sob uncontrollably. Molech motioned to his men to bring them back to the ladies room.

As the girls were being dragged back to the ladies room, six SWAT officers and their captain arrived at the warehouse. Wayne had formulated a plan of entry and all of the officers were taking their positions.

The man that Molech had sent to the office returned with a 12-gauge Remington 870 Express tactical shotgun. Molech clapped his hands once and the shotgun was tossed to him, upright, and he caught it with one hand.

The only thing stopping the officers from entering the building was an acknowledgement that the warrant to enter the building was signed.

"You know," Molech told Nice, "I was told you were coming." He then pumped the shotgun once. "But I wonder how the guy who told me, knew you were coming?"

Nice had no idea what he was talking about. The two men returned from the ladies room. Molech and his six men now faced Nice.

Nice reached into his tool bag and retrieved his Bible. He took the bag off his shoulder and set it on the ground. It appeared that Nice was surrendering to his fate as he stood there, Bible in hand, staring down at Molech.

Chelbi was also assessing the situation.

"Nice, I hear your sister," Chelbi blurted out.

Nice knew that line as a call to action. With one fist, he lunged and struck the man holding Chelbi, who immediately released his grip on her.

"RUN!" Nice screamed as he was now in a bare knuckle fist fight with all of the men, except Molech.

Chelbi raced to the last man door in the garage that she had not attempted to open. She planned to run into it at full speed like a runaway train. She hit it and the door opened. She slightly bounced to the outside of the building. The door closed and locked behind her.

Once outside, Wayne recognized her.

"Chelbi," Wayne called out and she promptly focused on his voice.

She ran to him hysterical, crying, and wanting to be hugged for a split second. She took a step back to look at him through her tears.

"Oh, my God, you've got to help him! They're gonna kill him!" Her message was urgent as she spoke with a cracking voice.

"Who?" Wayne responded with matched urgency.

"Nice," she responded, trying to hold back uncontrollable crying.

"Nicean?" Wayne asked.

"We were trying to help these girls in there."

As Chelbi completed her sentence, the unmistakable sound of a shotgun blast was heard from inside the building. Its resonance left a deadly pall over the landscape.

"Oh, God, they killed him!" she uttered with frenzied convulsion and a tempest of tears.

Like a quick cut in a movie, Wayne looked to the building and then back to SWAT Captain Hardiman.

"Give me your shotgun." It was not a request, it was a command.

Captain Hardiman was hesitant, but handed him the weapon. It was loaded with Disintegrator breaching rounds capable of destroying deadbolts, locks, and hinges.

"Wayne, wait!" Hardiman cautioned as Wayne walked to the door that Chelbi exited.

"Chelbi," Wayne told her as he stopped for a moment. "Stay with this detective," he said pointing to his partner, Andy Sandoval.

Wayne took the shotgun and moved briskly toward the building. As he approached it, he racked the shotgun by pumping it once. When he was within three feet of the door, he fired three shots at the door in quick succession, pumping it each time and turning his head away with each blast. The first blast was aimed at the locking mechanism of the door and the next two shots were aimed at the hinges of the door. Each shot blew apart its intended target. Wayne took one final shot at the center of the door, which blew the door and the doorframe into the building.

As Wayne rushed into the building, Captain Hardiman ordered the three SWAT teams to make entry.

Wayne entered a darkened loading area where tractor trailers would normally be parked. There were several parked vehicles at the far end of the building, including Molech's brown Toronado. Wayne could hear the other SWAT teams make entry and begin the process of clearing the building for any unfriendly combatants.

Darkness enveloped the room, except for the center of the loading area, approximately fifty feet from the door where Wayne had entered.

Sunlight shined down on Nice's frame and blond hair like a spotlight through the lone skylight in the ceiling. He looked confused and dirty, with a line of dried blood on his left cheek.

Wayne's voice refocused him.

"Nicean," Wayne called out. As he did, the other SWAT team members took aim at Nice and six red, laser dots filled his chest.

"Hold your fire!" Wayne yelled. "Get the lights!"

Wayne could see that Nice was holding something in his hand.

"Nice. What's in your hand?"

"My roadmap," he timidly responded.

"Drop it!" Wayne ordered.

Nice let go of the book in his hand and his Bible fell to the ground. As it fell, the lights came on, flooding the room with bright, clear illumination.

Less than ten feet from where Nice stood, lay the bodies of six men holding various handguns and Molech held a shotgun. Their condition was unknown, but they were not moving. There was no blood and no signs of blunt force trauma.

Wayne could see that Nice wore a blue t-shirt that had a hole in the center of the chest in the front and back of it. The back of the shirt appeared to be blood-soaked.

"Are you all right?" Wayne inquired with a concerned, elevated voice as he lowered his shotgun and began a slow creep toward Nice.

"Yeah," Nice answered.

"What happened here?"

Nice slowly perused the bodies and surveyed the carnage. He then turned to Wayne.

"A miracle."

CHAPTER 48

At the Carlsbad Police Station Headquarters, Nice sat in a sterile interrogation room waiting for Wayne. Nice had given his ripped and blood-soaked t-shirt to a crime lab technician and he was wearing a white t-shirt that Wayne gave to him.

Wayne entered, without his sport coat on, looking at Nice across a small, rectangular table. Wayne sat down and pulled his chair in closer to the table.

"Would you like something to drink?"

"No," Nice responded. "I'm fine."

"There're certain parts of your story that I would like to go over again."

Nice just looked at him. His face and hands were dirty and the wound that caused the line of dried blood on his face appeared to be healed.

"What happened to your face?" Wayne asked pointing to his own cheek.

"One of those guys hit me. I think he was wearing a ring."

"You know those guys are all dead?"

"I didn't know that," Nice answered without expression.

"When you were first confronted by these men, what did you do next?"

"I was carrying the two girls from the bathroom. They grabbed Chelbi. I put the girls down because I didn't want Chelbi to get hurt."

"What happened next?" Wayne asked with interest.

"I hit the guy who was holding Chelbi. He let her go. She ran out. I was in a fistfight trying to hold those guys off to make sure Chelbi got out. Then, the tall guy shot me."

"That's what I want to talk about," Wayne told him as he wiped a piece of lint off the table.

"It was a shotgun, right?" Nice nodded in agreement. "How far would you say the gun was from you when he pulled the trigger?"

"Three, maybe four, feet," Nice surmised.

"We found an expended shell for a 12-gauge shotgun. If you were shot from three to four feet away, it probably would have blown a hole in your chest," Wayne noted. "But as you can see, there's not a scratch on you. How do you explain that?"

"When I was hit, it felt like a cannon ball," Nice relayed. "I hit the ground and I was out."

"So, you woke up like this? Because the shirt you were wearing looked like you bled quite a bit." Wayne put his hand up to stop Nice before he answered. "Let's talk about when you woke up. Who was there?"

"I told you, it was a homeless guy that I saw earlier in the week. I gave him my lunch one day near the Jack-in-the-Box on Avenida Encinas and another time I gave him five dollars when I saw him on the northbound Poinsettia Drive freeway off-ramp."

"This guy just appeared out of nowhere?"

"I don't know. He was there when I woke up."

"Do you know where he went?"

"No. When you came through the door, I turned my attention to you. When I looked back, he was gone."

Wayne then interlaced his fingers and set them on the table.

"You know what I think, Nice," Wayne declared firmly. "I think there's more to the story. There were seven guys dead in there. Do you know how they died?"

"No, I don't." Nice was beginning to become irritated by the questions.

"There was no trauma to the bodies and no sign of blood loss. So, I'm thinking poison. Do you know anything about that?"

Nice stared at Wayne.

"No," Nice told him conclusively.

"Why did you need a machine gun?"

Nice let out a slight chuckle and leaned back in his chair.

"You really are a detective. I needed it for something that I was planning to do. Then, I found out I couldn't do it."

"What were you planning?" Wayne inquired.

"I wanted to go back in time and help Jesus on the day he was crucified. I thought the gun would help me persuade the Roman Army."

Wayne had no reaction to Nice's plan.

"Do you know the name Feardesin?"

"No."

"Molech?"

"That's a name mentioned in Leviticus, First and Second Kings, and, I think, Jeremiah. He's some sort of pagan god involved with child sacrifice."

"I want to ask you again, Nice. What happened to the men inside that warehouse today?"

Nice looked at Wayne with a stern visage and without emotion.

"Wayne, stop thinking like a cop. I know you're a religious man. You go to church every day and the other parishioners consider you a leader. *Are you faithful or are you faith full?*"

"I don't understand your question?"

"When you go to church, is it merely a mechanical exercise, where you react like a trained dog to give certain responses? Are you paying attention to what you're saying? Or, is it just rote memorization? When it's done, you don't even remember saying it. Are you listening to what Father Tom is saying? The bottom line is: Do you walk out of church different from the way you walk into it?" Nice stopped to let the statement sink in. "Think about it. Because you're right. There is *more* to the story."

Nice then pushed the chair back from the table and stood. At the same time, he could hear a dog barking in the distance and the volume indicated that the dog was getting closer. Nice recognized Yappy's bark.

"I believe I hear my sister calling me. Are you going to arrest me?"

Wayne was staring forward thinking about Nice's question to him.

"No," Wayne answered with a hint of despondency. "They're going to make you a hero."

"I'm not a hero. I'm a sinner. You shouldn't take credit for something that's the right thing to do. Peace be with you, Wayne."

Nice opened the door to the interrogation room and Yappy was performing her trademark dance on her hind legs. Nice picked her up and stroked her back as she rested against his shoulder and began licking his cheek.

"What are you doing, little girl?" he asked her. Then he heard his mother's voice.

"Nice, what happened?" she asked, somewhat in shock.

"I'll explain in the car, ma."

Nice and his family walked out of the police headquarters. Wayne sat in solitude, still thinking about what Nice said and what life was going to be like without his daughter.

CHAPTER 49

On this Saturday, slightly more than twenty-four hours after Wayne spoke with Nice in the Police interrogation room, Wayne and Marion Patterson sat quietly in the chapel at the Palomar Medical Center. It was peaceful and quiet. Marion admired the various paintings on the walls, while Wayne looked down and contemplated the events of the past week.

A janitor came into the chapel and began to empty a trash can near the door. The man pulled out the garbage bag and replaced it with a new one.

The janitor was sixty-four years old, heavyset, with dark skin and glasses. He wore a gray, long sleeve, button shirt and green trousers.

Marion spoke up to crack the silence.

"What was that verse that Joy picked out of your Bible?" she asked Wayne.

"It was from Mark, chapter 5, verse 23," Wayne noted with despondency. "I memorized it. *My little daughter lieth at the point of death. I pray thee, come and lay thy hands on her, that she may be healed; and she shall live.*"

Wayne took his right hand and lifted his glasses to rub his eyes. Marion reached for a tissue.

"That's not the complete verse," said a voice from the back of the room. The hospital's janitor wanted to comment on Wayne's Scripture reading.

"Excuse me," Wayne stood to look at him. Marion also turned to him.

"That verse begins with," the janitor informed them, "*And besought him greatly, saying*, then you got the rest of it right. Jairus, the guy speaking in that verse, went looking for Jesus."

The comment placed Wayne into deep thought. He looked down at Marion and then at the door.

"I'll be right back," he told Marion and ran out of the room.

Wayne was about to explore an epiphany he experienced. The epiphany of a desperate man taking desperate action.

CHAPTER 50

Nice's mother, Sally, and Yappy sat quietly in their living room, watching *Wheel of Fortune*. Just as the last commercial break of the episode began, there was an impatient rapping on the front door followed by three rings of the doorbell.

Sally wondered who was stopping by on a Saturday evening. She proceeded to the door and opened it. There stood Wayne.

"Wayne, come on in," she suggested.

"Is Nice here?"

Sally could tell from the speed and cadence of his voice that he was in a hurry.

"No. He's at Ben's."

"Okay. Sorry to bother you, Sally."

"How's Joy?" Sally asked with concern.

"Not good. Listen, I've got to go," Wayne conveyed and quickly retreated to his car.

"I'll pray for her," Sally announced to Wayne as he sped to his vehicle.

Within ten minutes, Wayne was at Ben's house. Again, he was knocking at the door with urgency and ringing the doorbell. Theresa, Ben's wife, answered the door.

"Wayne, how nice to see you. Where's Marion?" she inquired.

"She's at the hospital," Wayne told her with a rushed voice. "Is Nice here?"

"Yes. Come on in. He's watching TV with Ben and Chelbi."

"Thanks," Wayne acknowledged as he darted past her into their living room.

Ben, Nice, and Chelbi were watching the John Wayne movie, *The Searchers*. Ben and Nice had started to watch this movie on the previous Monday, but they were interrupted when Ben was informed that Chelbi was trying to buy drinks in a local bar. All three looked to Wayne as he dashed into the room.

"Hello, Wayne," Ben began a salutation, but was quickly cut off.

"Did he touch you?" Wayne stood there demanding an answer from Nice.

"Who?" Nice wondered about the question and why Wayne appeared so flummoxed.

"The man you saw in the warehouse yesterday. Did he touch you?" Wayne appeared to be growing impatient.

"Yes, he did. I was on the ground when I woke up. He took my hand and helped me to stand up."

"Can you come with me to the hospital right now?" Wayne asked.

"Why?" Nice replied.

"To pray," Wayne's voice started to crack. "To hold my daughter."

"Wayne, you don't have faith," Nice informed him. "You're driven by despair, not belief."

"No, Nice. That's why I'm here. I do believe. I do believe. I do believe."

"Are you trying to convince me or yourself?" Nice demanded.

"Nice," Ben's imposing figure quickly stood from his Barcalounger and looked at him with a stern countenance. "It's not for you to judge. If you won't do it for him, do it for me."

Nice looked at Ben, slightly overwhelmed by his outburst. He realized that he was wrong to have judged Wayne.

"Let's go," Nice told Wayne.

"I'm going too," Chelbi uttered.

The three of them raced to Wayne's unmarked police cruiser. They were about to set a new speed record for the trip between Ben's house and the Palomar Medical Center.

CHAPTER 51

When Nice, Wayne and Chelbi arrived at Joy's room at the Palomar Medical Center, Nice was overcome by her. All of her hair, including her eyebrows, was gone and her skin was pasty white. Her skin appeared to have powder makeup on it. She was gaunt and her trembling seemed to indicate an internal struggle to stay alive.

Wayne looked at Nice as if he wanted Nice to tell her to get up and walk. Nice took a moment to think about what to do.

"Please," Wayne begged.

Nice then moved into action. He moved to Joy's right side and started giving orders as if he was in a race against time.

"Wayne, get on that side," Nice told him, referring to the opposite side from Nice. "Touch the top of her head and her shoulder. Marion, stand next to Wayne and take her hand. Chelbi, come next to me and take her other hand."

Nice then placed his right hand on her forehead and his left hand under her head.

Wayne, Chelbi, and Marion looked at Nice for further direction.

"Wayne, lead us in prayer," Nice commanded.

"Shouldn't you do it?" Wayne asked.

"No. Do it."

Wayne took a deep breath and began.

"Our father, who,"

"NO!" Nice cut him off with caustic rage. "Do *The Profession of Faith*."

"I don't know it," Wayne feared.

"You have been saying it for over fifty years. You *do* know it, Wayne! Because you are *faith full*."

Wayne wanted to believe him.

"I believe in one God," Wayne began, "the Father almighty, maker of heaven and earth, of all things visible and invisible."

As Wayne continued to speak, the words initially had no effect on his daughter.

"I believe in one Lord Jesus Christ, the Only Begotten Son of God, born of the Father before all ages. God from God, Light from Light, true God from true God, begotten, not made, consubstantial with the Father; through him all things were made."

Joy then began to react, but it was not the desired reaction. She began to convulse as if she was having a seizure. Wayne stopped.

"Don't stop!" Nice barked the order. "Come on, 'For us men,'" Nice said referring to the next line of the prayer.

Wayne continued sheepishly.

"For us men and for our salvation he came down from heaven, and by the Holy Spirit was incarnate of the Virgin Mary, and became man."

Chelbi's voice then interrupted him.

"Her blood pressure's dropping."

"Wayne, I'm telling you, DON'T STOP! FINISH THE PRAYER!"

Wayne again began.

"For our sake he was crucified under Pontius Pilate, he suffered death and was buried, and rose again on the third day in accordance with the Scriptures."

Joy began to convulse dramatically. An alarm went off from the machine that was monitoring her vital signs. Wayne continued the prayer.

"He ascended into heaven and is seated at the right hand of the Father. He will come again in glory to judge the living and the dead and his kingdom will have no end."

Marion and Chelbi stared at Joy's blood pressure and pulse readings. Nice looked at the monitor for a moment, then looked to the doorway. It was then that Nice's face changed. It turned from caring to enraged.

"Everybody, join with Wayne," Nice directed as he continued to eye the doorway.

In unison, they proceeded.

"I believe in the Holy Spirit, the Lord, the giver of life, who proceeds from the Father and the Son, who with the Father and the Son is adored and glorified, who has spoken through the prophets."

The alarm on the vital signs monitor was now cacophonous, nearly drowning out their four voices. But no hospital personnel were responding. They reached the final line of the prayer. Nice kept his focus on the doorway.

"I believe in one, holy, catholic and apostolic Church. I confess one Baptism for the forgiveness of sins and I look forward to the resurrection of the dead and the life of the world to come. Amen."

As they uttered the word, 'Amen,' the noise from the machine stopped for a millisecond, followed by the sound associated with a flatline heart stoppage event.

Nice was shocked and Marion began to cry.

"NOOOOOOOOO!" Wayne screamed at the top of his lungs and fell to his knees. His voice resonated in the room, the hallway, and the entire sixth floor of the hospital.

CHAPTER 52

EVENTS AFTER CHELBI
RAN OUT OF THE WAREHOUSE

Nice was held by two of Molech's henchmen while being pummeled by another. One right hook to his face cut a line across his cheek and blood started to run.

"That's enough," Molech proclaimed. "Let him go."

The two men holding Nice stepped back from him. Molech looked him in the eye and in one moment, leveled the shotgun and pulled the trigger. The sound of the exploding shell resonated within the interior of the cavernous warehouse.

The shotgun was less than three feet from Nice's body when it was fired. The impact of the shotgun pellets hit him directly in the center of the chest, lifting him up off his feet and flying him through the air approximately eight feet away where his body slammed to the concrete floor.

The shot put a five inch hole in the center of Nice's chest. It ripped through his ribs, internal organs, including his heart, and his spine. Nice was dead when he hit the floor. In his hand, he continued to hold his Bible.

Molech and his men turned to walk to the ladies room, when they heard what sounded like footsteps. They looked back and there stood a man, 5 feet 11 inches tall, 170 pounds, in his early 30s, with longer, curly, brown hair, beard and moustache. He was the same homeless man that Nice had seen earlier in the week at the Jack-in-the-Box restaurant and on the freeway off-ramp.

The man's complexion glowed and his green eyes were mesmerizing. He wore a white tunic made from one square of cloth. The tunic had two brown stripes that ran from shoulder to hem. He also wore a mantle, which was a large, rectangular cloth that he wrapped around himself. On his feet were the same sandals that Nice saw him wearing earlier in the week.

As soon as Molech saw him, he pumped the shotgun, expending the round that killed Nice and loading another round in the chamber of the gun.

As Molech racked the weapon, the man held out the three middle fingers of his right hand, slightly higher than his head, and gently moved them from right to left. All seven of the men immediately fell to the ground. It was as if the electricity within them was turned off.

The man then walked over to Nice and knelt down next to him on one knee. He placed both of his hands over the hole in Nice's chest. At that moment, it was as if a billion cells came to life and the area that was blown out of Nice's chest regenerated. Even the cut on his cheek was healed. The man then lightly touched him on the cheek and his eyes opened.

Nice was slightly startled, wondering where he was. But when he saw the homeless man, he knew that he was in the presence of the Almighty.

"Hello, Nice," the man said with a smile. "Peace be with you."

"And with you," Nice uttered in a wondrous tone.

The man stood and extended his hand to Nice, who grabbed it with an arm wrestling grip, and he was pulled up to his feet. Nice just looked at him with pure joy.

"I was supposed to come and help you," he said sincerely.

"You did," the man replied. "What you do for the least of my brothers and sisters, you do for me." A moment passed. "Do you understand now?"

"I do."

The sound of shotgun blasts could be heard as Wayne was about to breach the door.

"Don't forget me," Nice said.

"A Father can never forget his child, my son."

As he uttered that line, the door burst open from Wayne's final shotgun blast. Nice turned to watch the door fly in. When he looked back, the man was gone.

EPILOGUE

LEGOLAND CALIFORNIA
9 YEARS LATER

At the Carlsbad, California theme park, this day was Uniform Appreciation Day. Military personnel, veterans, police officers, members of the fire department, and any uniformed occupation that provided service to the public was given free admittance for the entire family.

Chelbi and Betty Rondolay used the opportunity to plan a social outing for what they referred to as their family. Ben was a veteran, so he was able to get free tickets and Wayne, who retired shortly after the events at the Semany Warehouse, was now involved with the Carlsbad Police Benevolent Association and was able to obtain tickets for everyone invited by Chelbi and Betty.

The lines were long to get in, but Ben now used a scooter, so everyone was able to enter quickly through the handicap access line. Ben drove a red, electric Spitfire scooter, which allowed him to zip around unimpeded.

Nice and Chelbi had been married for six years now and they had three children, whom Betty referred to as "my babies." Their children were named Benjamin, Sally, and Betty, in honor of the three people who had the greatest influence on their lives.

Nice took over Ben's Glassworks with Diz and a couple of new people. Lozo moved to Oregon in the hope of finding a more affordable lifestyle. Ben was still around for advice and counsel. Nice would stop by Ben's house every day to see if Ben and Theresa needed anything.

Betty was still a 'Georgia Peach," but she was not as jovial as she once was. Her husband, Bob, died suddenly three years earlier and she continues to grieve for him.

Sally and Yappy were there. Sally was moving slower and Yappy, now eleven-years-old with more white hair around her mouth, would still bark up a storm if anyone came near Sally. This day, she was accompanied by her sister, Marie Mitchell, from Great Falls, Montana. Marie was ten years younger than Sally, also petite and finely dressed. She carried a two-year-old, black and gray, toy schnauzer terrier named Rhett. This boy dog looked just like Yappy nine years earlier. Both dogs wore a white collar with the word, 'SERVICE,' printed on it in red.

Before moving on to any of the attractions, they waited for Wayne and Marion. Ben offered to go out to the parking lot to find them and then bring them in through the handicap entrance. Before any steps had to be taken to find them, a familiar voice was heard.

"Nice," Wayne called over to him and waved.

"Wayne's here," Nice announced to the group.

"Sorry, we're late," Wayne said. "We had to stop for a bathroom break." He looked back and saw Marion attempting to make her way through the crowd. As Marion drew closer, Nice recognized the woman who accompanied her. It was their daughter, Joy.

As soon as Joy saw Nice, she went directly up to him and gave him a tight hug and a kiss on the cheek. In his ear, she said, "Peace be with you."

When she let go of Nice and stepped back, Nice told her, "And also with you." Nice had seen Joy on a semi-regular basis over the past nine years and it was always a pleasure. He believed her existence was a testament to the power of prayer.

Joy was married seven years earlier and now had four children, ranging in age from three months to six years. Her husband was a pediatrician in San Diego and he was unable to join her this day.

Wayne was prepared with strollers, as was Betty and Chelbi.

"Should we get going, y'all?" Chelbi said making Betty proud of her influence on her.

Before heading to the various rides, Joy introduced her children to Marie, Sally's sister. All the children were infatuated with Rhett and Yappy.

Joy's six-year-old son, Billy, had a quick question for his mother before moving on. It was within earshot of Nice.

"Who is that man, mommy?"

"He's the man who saved me," Joy shared with her son.

Billy looked at Nice as his mother led him away. And Nice began to remember.

It was the night when Nice and Chelbi raced to the hospital to pray for Joy as she battled death for survival. Nice recalled how Joy began to convulse dramatically. An alarm went off from the machine that was monitoring her vital signs. Wayne continued the prayer.

"He ascended into heaven and is seated at the right hand of the Father. He will come again in glory to judge the living and the dead and his kingdom will have no end."

Marion and Chelbi stared at Joy's blood pressure and pulse readings. Nice looked at the monitor for a moment, then looked to the doorway. Nice's face changed, turned from caring to enraged.

What enraged him was the figure of a man, 6 feet tall, on a large frame. He was dressed in a black suit, with a black shirt and tie, wrap-around sunglasses, black gloves, and a black fedora. His facial features were indistinguishable as he was cloaked in the darkness of the hallway. Nice knew who it was. It was Feardesin.

"Everybody, join with Wayne," Nice directed as he continued to eye the doorway.

As they proceeded in unison with the prayer, the alarm on the vital signs monitor was now cacophonous, nearly drowning out their four voices. But no hospital personnel were responding. They reached the final line of the prayer. Nice kept his focus on the doorway.

As Joy's deterioration continued to accelerate, Feardesin broadcast a smile, with his yellowed, rotted teeth, now on display. He then reached for his sunglasses and removed them. In his eyes, fire appeared to be within his eye sockets.

As Nice, Wayne, Marion, and Chelbi finished the prayer by uttering the word, 'Amen,' the noise from the machine stopped and the sound associated with a flatline heart stoppage event filled the air.

Nice saw the smile on Feardesin's face suddenly evaporate and turn to one of wrenching pain. Feardesin now began to tremble and suddenly, burst into black smoke.

At that moment, through the smoke came a doctor who walked in just as Wayne let out his agonizing and arduous scream.

"NOOOOOOOOO!" Wayne shrieked.

"It looks like the machine had a little malfunction," the doctor told them. "Just need to reset it."

The doctor walked directly to the vital signs monitor and clicked a button in the back of it to turn it off and then on. He then took his left hand and touched Joy on the shoulder with his three middle fingers. Her blood pressure and pulse returned to normal.

Nice witnessed the events and spoke up before the doctor left the room.

"Excuse me, doctor." The doctor stopped and turned to look at him. "Do I know you?"

"Anything's possible," he replied, then continued on his path out the door.

Nice knew it was the homeless man from the warehouse the day before. Now clean-shaven and dressed like a doctor. Nice quickly went out to the hallway to follow him, but he was gone.

Nice thought about that day every time he said *The Profession of Faith* prayer. He knew that he was not the one who saved Joy that day, he merely helped Wayne find his faith and the light.

Back at LEGOLAND, Nice sat on a bench, talking with Ben, while the women and all the children were waiting in line for the Fairy Tale Brook ride.

"Hey, Nice," Ben called out to get his attention. "What are we going to do here today? Where do they have those Granny's Apple Fries?"

"I think up by the castle," Nice said with a smile. Ben just arrived and he was already bored.

"We got to check those out," Ben told him.

"You guys from around here?" a man, sitting next to Nice, asked.

"Yeah," Nice responded. "We live just a couple of miles away."

"Is the weather always like this here? We're from Libertyville, Illinois and I'm ready to move."

"The weather is always like this, warm and breezy," Nice responded without hesitation.

"What's Carlsbad like?" the man asked.

Nice looked at Ben, then looked to his family and Joy standing in line for the ride, before answering his question.

"It's the place where God goes on vacation."

Appendix A

THE PROFESSION OF FAITH

(Nicene Creed)

I believe in one God,
 the Father almighty,
maker of heaven and earth,
 of all things visible and invisible.

I believe in one Lord Jesus Christ,
 the Only Begotten Son of God,
 born of the Father before all ages.
 God from God, Light from Light,
 true God from true God,
 begotten, not made, consubstantial with the Father;
 through him all things were made.
 For us men and for our salvation
 he came down from heaven,
 and by the Holy Spirit was incarnate of the Virgin Mary,
 and became man.
 For our sake he was crucified under Pontius Pilate,
 he suffered death and was buried,
 and rose again on the third day
 in accordance with the Scriptures.
 He ascended into heaven
 and is seated at the right hand of the Father.
 He will come again in glory
 to judge the living and the dead
 and his kingdom will have no end.

I believe in the Holy Spirit, the Lord, the giver of life,
who proceeds from the Father and the Son,
who with the Father and the Son is adored and glorified,
who has spoken through the prophets.

I believe in one, holy, catholic and apostolic Church.
I confess one Baptism for the forgiveness of sins
and I look forward to the resurrection of the dead
and the life of the world to come. Amen.

About the Author

Vince Aiello grew up in upstate New York before moving to Southern California where he attended California Western School of Law. He is admitted to practice law in both New York and California. *Faith Full* is his fourth novel. His earlier legal thriller novels, *Legal Detriment*, *The Litigation Guy*, and *Legion's Lawyers* were all acclaimed bestsellers. Visit his website at www.vinceaiello.com.

ACKNOWLEDGEMENTS

I would like to thank the following individuals for providing support and, in some instances, the use of their name for a fictional character in *Faith Full*:

Ethan P. Aiello
Sarah Rose Aiello
Valerie R. Aiello, RPh
Angelo Garubo, Esq.
Troy Geisser, Esq.
Fr. Donald Coleman
Ben Krische
Theresa Krische
Fr. William Marquis
Marie Mitchell
Rhett (the dog) Mitchell
Marion Patterson
Wayne Patterson
Chelbi Gorringe Stubbs
Pat Sullivan

www.ingramcontent.com/pod-product-compliance
Lightning Source LLC
Chambersburg PA
CBHW061158170626
46809CB00003B/1153